THE FACADE

WE ALL HAVE A STORY, WE WISH WASN'T TRUE

Edited & Compiled by

Rashi Aggarwal

Inkfeathers Publishing

First Published in India in 2020
Inkfeathers Publishing
New Delhi 110095

ISBN 978-81-946199-9-4

www.inkfeathers.com

Co-Authored By

CF Gonzi ~ Hari Pudipeddi ~ Shel Henderson ~ Snehal Agarwal ~ Dr. Anuraag Awasthi ~ Kriti ~ Adyasha Mishra ~ Rashi Aggarwal ~ Colby Hobson ~ Suraj Singh Sisodia ~ Srishti Sareen ~ Ayush Aggarwal

DISCLAIMER

The anthology "The Facade" is a collection of stories by 12 authors who belong to different parts of the globe. The anthology editor and the publisher have edited the content provided by the co-authors to enhance the experience for readers and make it free of plagiarism as much as possible. All the stories published in this anthology are a work of fiction. Unless otherwise indicated, all the names, characters, objects, businesses, places, events, incidents- whether physical/non-physical, real/unreal, tangible/intangible in whatsoever description used in this book are either the product of the author's imagination or used in a fictitious manner. Any resemblance to actual persons, objects, entities, living or dead, or actual events is purely coincidental. The stories published in this book are solely owned by their respective authors and are no way intended to hurt anyone's religious, political, spiritual, brand, personal or fanatic beliefs and/or faith, whatsoever.

In case, any sort of plagiarism is detected in the stories within this anthology or in case of any complaints or grievances or objections, neither the anthology editor, nor the publisher are to be held responsible for any such claims. The author(s) who holds the rights to the particular story, shall be held responsible, whatsoever.

CONTENTS

ABOUT THE EDITOR

RASHI AGGARWAL

Rashi is an International Business and Finance Graduate. Despite her corporate career, she has a profound passion for art, culture and literature. She believes in learning constantly and not limiting skills and knowledge to one's career. She graduated in classical dance along with her business degree and now is studying fine arts too. She fell in love with literature quite early in her life. Her first book was "Bubble's First Storybook" which her mother read to her every day. She soon discovered the world of classical literature and read avidly. She frequently participated in literary events and quizzes. Her first blog was on WordPress on which she wrote philosophical fiction under a pen name. When one of her posts got really popular and was shared widely, it motivated her to publish her first book on Amazon Kindle. She has written under her pen name since the recent year. She also worked at KPMG India as a Project Trainee where she was responsible for third party marketing through content creation, digital creatives and social media management. She is working on her next novel which she soon wishes to publish under her real name.

EDITOR'S NOTE

As I live in Delhi, the commute time to any place is pretty long. I prefer to use Delhi Metro over driving by myself because at that time I get to read, think, work on my draft or talk to fellow travellers. It is a major inspiration behind the characters in my stories. One day, while I was on the way to my workplace, I was thinking about the word "facade" and how this one simple word has a powerful metaphorical aspect to it. A facade literally means the front of a building but metaphorically means a masquerade for someone's pretence. That's how I stumbled upon the idea for this book. I believe the world is full of illusions and so are people. A person who seems regular might be living a different reality on the inside. The ideology was to put forward the stories about how someone's facade could be diabolical.

I kept working on this idea and decided to write a few short stories by myself. But it wasn't going in the direction I hoped for and soon the project was abandoned. It was just a dead folder in my laptop until I came across the anthology concept by Inkfeathers Publishing. I pitched them the idea and it soon got approved. That was one of the happiest moments in my life. Inkfeathers Publishing provided me with an amazing platform to implement this idea and make it into a real book.

I am grateful to all the co-authors of this book who spun eccentric, whimsical tales from their vivid imagination. I never imagined that the theme could be perceived in such distinct ideologies which are wildly creative and impressive. The stories range from contrasting genres like romance to horror, supernatural to contemporary fiction, and so on. It is quite astonishing how the stories follow a similar theme and yet differ in perception. The idea is to appeal to everyone's literary tastes and preferences. All the authors worked on this project with great enthusiasm and resilience. With their timely submission, I was able to compile this anthology on time. I am glad I got the opportunity to network with such talented people who helped me to make this project into a wonderful and unique anthology.

Once again, I present my gratitude to everyone who was involved in this project.

THE FACADE

WE ALL HAVE A STORY, WE WISH WASN'T TRUE

STORY ONE

THE ONLY RIGHT CHOICE

by CF Gonzi

If we take the Hylain Route," I traced my finger down the map lying on the table, "There should be an entrance used by the dwarves on the south end of the wall."

Odette's sad eyes stared at me quizzically. "The Hylain Route is heavily trafficked by the dwarves, not to mention the merchants and elves that use it as a shortcut in the night to travel between kingdoms."

She stood, grasping my rough hand in her slender fingers and putting my palm above the little hand-drawn castle. "Don't you think the Northam Pass would be the better option here? Yusav's told us again and again that the kingdom's wall is low and unguarded near there."

Yusav was Odette's younger brother; he had been jumping the kingdom's wall to bring us food and supplies since the day we were banished.

I picked at the skin peeling on my lower lip. She had a point, I guess. It would be better to avoid contact with anyone, whether they were leaving or entering the city. And since there was no entrance near the Northam Pass, it was almost guaranteed we could scale the wall undetected. I began to nod slowly before smiling up at her.

"How did I get so lucky?" I pulled her down onto my lap, kissing her pale lips and running my hand through her silver hair. "My wife is a better strategist than myself."

"Hmm." Odette nibbled my lip softly before she pulled away. "I wonder about that every day."

"Ha-ha." I gently ran my fingers down her sides, making her tremble and jump out of my reach. I laughed genuinely this time. "We can go tonight."

"If you think it best." She stared at the floor.

I stood, placing her chin gently between my finger and thumb and lifting her amethyst eyes to meet mine.

"We can do this. And just think, when we do, we can bring her back to us."

I think the most devastating scene in the world is that of an elf crying. I wiped away Odette's tears, as heart-wrenchingly beautiful as they were, and pulled her into my chest. *The next brilliant tears she cries*, I thought, *will be those of happiness.*

"Shall we prepare then?" Odette looked up at me, brushing a stray strand of hair behind her pointed ear.

"Indeed, but first. . ." I stooped down to kiss her again, her slim and graceful body relaxing in my arms as our lips met. I closed my eyes. There wasn't a day gone by that I didn't marvel at my fortune of having an elf for a wife. She was everything I ever wanted, and I wished I could freeze moments like these and live in them forever.

But, unfortunately, that wish had yet to come true. Odette pulled out of the embrace, breathing heavily and shaking her head.

"Is this really the time, Arc?" she smiled at me. "Why don't you prepare the bag while I go check that everything is in order for Yusav to stay with Estella."

When did I get to the point where just the mere sound of her name sent a dagger into my heart?

"Er, yes, that would be good." I turned away as Odette left the room, trying to focus on the map once more.

Estella was our daughter, the most beautiful and intelligent child I had ever laid eyes on. But she was also the most ill.

It had taken Odette and me eight years to conceive, most likely due to the fact that she was an elf and I a human. Estella was born in this very shack and was as wide-eyed and silent as she is now, nine months later. She had only ever been able to move her eyes since the day she was born; every other limb and body part had remained dormant. A physician from the kingdom was permitted to come and see us after the delivery, thanks to the begging and bothering done by Yusav, and told us Estella was afflicted with an unknown illness. There was no diagnosis, but there was an assumption that she would not live a full year.

That was the second time I had to watch my lovely wife cry, and it was the first time she had seen me shed a tear. We felt life could not have dealt us a more bitter hand. First banished because we refused to deny our love for each other, and now a child that was destined to die. We were the embodiment of the saying: "Life is unfair".

Life would be fair if that tyrant wasn't in charge, I thought bitterly as I rolled the map up and stuffed it in my satchel. King Bazric had made interracial marriage explicitly illegal the day of his coronation. Unless they petitioned for divorcement right away, anyone married to someone outside their race would be banished. Interracial marriage was already a scarce occurrence, but his awful decree abolished it completely. Odette and I had courted before King Bazric's reign began, and after refusing to cancel the engagement, we were one of the three couples who were banished. The first time I had to watch those crystal tears fall from Odette's beautiful eyes was when we waved goodbye to our families at the gate.

I decided then that Bazric was no king.

My hands trembled as I put the satchel beside our cloaks. Everything was in order for us to leave tonight. My chest tightened as I glanced at the ripped blanket that separated Estella's room from the rest of our shack. I took a deep breath. I was saying my temporary goodbye for a good reason.

Yusav was not as slender as the rest of the elves; his broad back was blocking Estella from my view as I entered the room.

"And then the frog said, 'Well, I'm just a little jumpy!'" Yusav read before slapping his knee jovially. "Get it, Stelly? Because frogs jump. *Ribbit*!"

"You're too good at that." I smiled, patting his shoulder and walking around to see my baby. Her eyes, as purple as her mother's, quickly met mine, and we were connected.

"I mean, talking with them makes them easier to imitate." Yusav stood and rubbed the back of his neck, his pale skin turning pink.

"I believe it. Thanks for reading to her," I knelt by her cradle, careful not to blink. If you blinked while she was locked onto you, she would look away. I never wanted her to look away. "Do you know where Odette went?"

"She told me she was going to the well to gather extra water for us during my stay."

"Good, good." I was hearing but not really listening. There was something about being near Estella—something that made it entirely impossible to focus on anything else.

"Er, Arc?"

He made me blink. Estella looked away, and I tried hard not to swear.

"What?"

"Are you sure you want to go through with this?"

I stroked Estella's cheek, trying to get her to look at me again. "Yes."

"You are no thief."

"I will be what I need to be," I didn't want to have this conversation with Yusav; it had already taken a fortnight to convince Odette. "Will you please leave us so I may say goodbye?"

"Of course." I heard the tattered blanket swish as Yusav stomped out.

"He doesn't understand, my sweet," I stroked Estella's dark hair. She had gotten that from me. "He doesn't know what it is like to be a father. I can't lose you."

Her wide eyes locked onto mine once more. She squinted slightly.

"Now, don't give me that," I clasped her cold, tiny hand. "The Vidain Orb is the only thing that can keep you with me. You don't want to go so soon, right?"

Her pupils dilated slightly as her vibrant irises glossed over.

“Bazric doesn’t deserve to hold that power.” I knew Estella would understand once she was cured. “This is all that fool’s fault anyway.”

Estella’s eyes jumped to the entrance of the room, and I turned around quickly. Odette stood watching us, a small smile on her perfect lips. Estella blinked.

“Well, we’ve got to go, love,” I kissed her pale forehead, putting my hand on her little belly. “We’ll be back before you know it.”

Odette was silent as we exited our shack. I watched her out of the corner of my eye as we made our way toward the kingdom that had kicked us out. Odette had refused to go through with my plan for quite some time. She said that the Vidain Orb was the source of all the life in the kingdom, and if we removed it, the agricultural ecosystem would be destroyed. She told me that my hatred for Bazric had blinded me.

After weeks of pleading, Odette had finally agreed that Bazric wasn’t fit to rule and that the power was better entrusted to someone who needed it. To us.

We reached the Northam Pass much quicker than I anticipated. Odette hadn’t said a single word. She was probably nervous. I was hoping to leave her out of this, but her flora magic should prove useful in scaling the kingdom’s walls and getting me inside the castle.

We approached a side of the wall that was much lower than the rest, maybe only 10 feet above the sandy path. I turned to Odette, holding her face in my hands. She grabbed my wrists gently.

“I love you.” She whispered.

“I love you too.” I stroked her cheek. “Are you ready?”

Odette nodded slowly before stepping back and closing her eyes. I always loved to watch her connect with the earth. Our chance at survival after being banished was greatly increased because of the magic Odette had been endowed with. And as I watched the shimmering vines wind up the wall like snakes, I was again awestruck with the phenomenal power her elven blood had granted her.

"Alright," her bright eyes reflected the moon as she opened them. "Now the drop shouldn't be too far on the other side. Arc?"

"Yes?" I grabbed the nearest vine, looking up at the wall.

"Are you sure about this?"

I clenched my jaw and started climbing. She already knew I wouldn't change my mind. I heard her sigh as the vine beside me started swaying. At least she was still going to come with me.

The Northam Pass was not only the best option for lack of surveillance but for the close proximity, it was to the actual castle. As I dropped from the vine, I glared up at the silhouette of the massive palace. Bazric didn't deserve any of this. No one here did if they believed that love between races was incorrect. Taking the Orb would not only save my Estella but bring an incredible vengeance to those who ruined our lives. It was the only right choice.

There was absolutely no one to be seen in this far corner of the kingdom, and I signaled for Odette to follow me. Staying in the shadow of the wall we had just jumped, I stalked silently to the left till I saw a window, about halfway up the massive stone stronghold. One more time. Odette only needed to help one more time, and then she could stay here, and I would take on the most dangerous part alone.

Her entrancing vines started creeping up the wall without me even asking. I glanced back, watching her fingers tremble as she summoned such strong vines as to hold me. Opening her glistening eyes when she finished, she grabbed my hand, as if to stop me. I squeezed tightly before letting go and turning once again to the cursed castle. The plan from here on was for me to go alone.

Lowering myself was much easier than pulling me up. Gravity could do most of the work, and after a quick pause in the window to ensure the coast was clear, I dropped down casually.

"That's far enough."

I froze.

"Arc, Banished Son of Morpheus, you are under arrest for the attempted thievery of the Vidain Orb."

I turned slowly, somehow completely surrounded by castle guards, the leader of which stood right in front of me with his sword drawn.

I unsheathed my own, pouncing at the nearest soldier. His weapon slipped easily from his grasp, but my triumph was short-lived as the head guard parried my next attack, sending my sword flying. Soldiers caved in, wrestling my arms to my sides.

"How would you know what I came for?" I spat at the leader's feet, straining against the hands pinning me down.

"Let's just say a little birdie told us." His smirk made my blood boil, but then he stepped to the side.

"Odette?" My voice was weak. Odette stood among the palace soldiers, her impossibly perfect face streaked with tears.

"Arc, please—"

"No," I whispered, looking down. "No."

"You've changed, Arc—"

"*No*!" I yelled. Odette flinched, and my knees buckled. "Why?"

She sobbed, and I had to hold her. I struggled against the guards keeping me down.

"You really think our daughter's life is more important than an entire kingdom? Than our families and friends?"

I slumped to the ground, desperate tears stinging my eyes as I stared up at her.

"You don't?"

STORY TWO

THE VISITOR

by Hari Pudipeddi

I open the door and quietly step into the living room. I don't need the lights - I know my way around this house. My visit is not going to be long unless the old boy resists and fights back again.

I stroll across the dining area and through the kitchen to the back door. I take a peek at the backyard and a memory flashes in my head.

It was forty-six summers ago that I came here for the first time. To take away with me the eldest son of this house. He fell off a mango tree and landed his head on a granite. Bleeding, he lay there for a long time - his throat croaking with thirst; unable to scream - before his younger brother saw the blood and screamed. His mother came, followed her second son's eyes, and ran crying out loud and fell down beside her bleeding son. The younger one went in to get water at her mother's command, while she held the elder one in her lap. Her eyes widened to large circles as her sari got washed in red. She fainted.

I saw this whole procession from atop the tree, waiting for life to leave the boy; for my time to set in so that I can claim him and go home.

I saw the younger boy come out with a bottle of water. I saw him collapse down to a sitting position beside his mother and brother, and stare blankly in bewildered innocence and fear. I remember him wetting his pants. I remember him crying, and screaming, and shouting, pleading for his brother to wake up. He didn't.

I sensed life slipping away and climbed down the tree.

The sun was setting when a man came searching for his family and found them all three in the backyard.

That was my first encounter with him, the six-foot-tall, handsome, shiny brown son of a bitch, whom I visited many times later to take away with me, but he ditched me every single time. As many as four times in the forty-six summers to come.

He was either lucky, strong, or brave and fought with courage all those times, but that day – the day I came not for him but the blood of his – he was weak. He was dead only then in all the eighty-six summers he has been through so far.

I do not remember much else from that day. There were lots of people – neighbours and relatives - in the house. But the last image I remember as I left with the boy is of this man – the father – sitting all alone in a chair in the living room, crying silently and helplessly into his hands.

I had completed my duty. He had lost his son.

***

I come back inside and pass through the arch from the dining area into the living room. I walk into a corridor beyond the stairs on the right and find two doors opposite to each other – just as I remember from another visit, in another time. Since my first visit to this house, the bedroom on the left remained empty. I knew it the moment I came back here some eighteen summers after the first visit.

I was on another job. There was going to be another life leaving a human body and I was there to claim it. That human body belonged to the younger brother of the boy I took away many years earlier from this same house.

Blood of the old man who is right now sleeping upstairs.

I open the door on my right and go in.

That second visit was short.

I knew from a week before about my duty here in this house. I knew of the horrors that were going through the mind of the human I was about to take – I was wired to it. There were voices in his head that blamed him for his brother's death. They convinced him. They made him believe that he was a failure. A loser.

I didn't know if the voices were there for a long time, but only around then they intensified. Screaming and croaking and crying and shouting and billowing, they rang in my ears too.

A week later I was there sitting on a bench across the street. When the time came, I went through the main door, came into this very room, and watched the younger brother – now a young man – tie a rope to the ceiling. I watched him drag the bed out of the way. Then he was gone for a while. When he came back, he was carrying a tall stool. He stood on it, and slipped the noose around his neck and kicked the stool from under.

It was over in a jiffy.

I waited and watched life seep away from his eyes.

As I left, I saw this man again, coming back home along with his wife, smiling and happy, unaware of another bundle of grief I had bestowed on him.

Now I see the bed, unslept, unmade; I see the dust settled on furniture; I see rats running around; I sense a presence and a memory of mine – the one I didn't know of until now – in that room, in that corridor. A smell of me from my past days lingers here; it stinks. And I feel the urge to get out of there.

I am scared for the first time, of myself. Of the rooms I have emptied of life.

As I stand in the doorway of the house, sunlight slowly starts penetrating the house through the windows.

And I know the time is up. It can be anytime now.

So I turn and start up the stairs.

By the time I reach the first floor, all the times I failed against this man flash in my head. Memories. Bad memories. Of the times he escaped me.

The first time was immediately after I took their elder son away. He was still trying to cope with the fresh wound in his heart, perhaps. I didn't care.

On the twelfth day after seeing him for the first time, I was waiting at a junction two streets away from his house. He was going to cross the street, dazed and lost, and get hit by a truck.

Was supposed to, anyway.

The brakes of the truck failed and the driver was drunk.

It had to be the day – that first time – but just before he could step onto the road to cross, a man tapped him on his shoulder and he turned around.

I got out of there.

Six months later, at a carnival, he was about to get onto a Giant Wheel which was going to fail and collapse. I was there. I took thirty-three men and women with me that day. But he wasn't in them. Just before he was about to get on, his son puked. Result of the Roller Coaster ride he just came off.

The husband and wife took him away.

And I went back again without him.

I reach the landing and look around. Here it is very dark. As dark as the footprints I left behind everywhere I went. It has been ten summers since I was here on this floor. And I try to think back to that memory.

I sat in the living room and watched the once mother and wife of this house faint, and fall down the stairs, landing on the marbled floor with a loud thud, followed by a scream.

Then the same man - who eluded me thrice until then - was by her side. I followed them to the hospital. And waited there. I knew of the life declining in her day by day. I saw it decrease to half when she fell. But a few men in white coats tried hard. A week later, they sent her back. She was to remain in bed. I had to stay by the bedside. All the time.

They brought her back from the hospital on a stretcher and took her up the stairs. At the landing on the first floor, they turned right and went on. At the end of the corridor, they turned yet another right and on the immediate left, there was the door.

I followed in through the door.

I stayed there, for a whole week. All the time of the day and night.

And one midnight, life gave up, and I went home.

***

I open and slip through the same door again now.

There is a lamp burning by the bed, showing his face in a glow of orange. I see his calm sleeping face and think to myself, "He isn't going to come even today."

But somewhere there was hope.

I settle myself down in a chair in the corner – the same one I sat in the last time.

And watch.

Sixteen summers ago. This same man slept here. And made me sit in the same chair I was to sit again after six summers. And another ten summers later once again.

He slept and life left him day after day. There were things, blood termites, sucking him dry from inside. There were men in white coats every day. He insisted on sleeping here, in his bedroom - where he slept all his life - for the last sleep too, when it did come.

He didn't know I - his last sleep - was sitting there with him.

He cried and wretched and groaned every day in pain. Pain from being eaten away.

After sitting there for sixty-three days and nights, I saw enough life fill him day after day. All the life I saw leaving him, just came back bit by bit.

He defeated cancer – one of the many aliases I was called by.

The old fuck won over me again.

***

He makes me wait.

I cannot leave until I take him or until he beats me; until I see life staying back.

I see none of it.

He moves, just a little jerk of his hand and a small movement of legs, and then he goes still again.

I wait.

And just when I get restless, a half-hour later, deciding that this one's also going to be long, he jerks yet again, and this time his hand moves to his chest. Tries to clutch, but gives up.

Hand falls. His chest stops rising.

The breathing stops.

Life calmly escapes out through his belly button.

I see all this as I have seen many times previously. In many other visits to many other people.

I look at his face.

With a smile on it, he raises his hand - for me.

My body turns cold and the crack on my lips flattens as I take his hand.

STORY THREE

TURNING OF ABIGAIL FROST- WHITE ROOM

by Shel Henderson

There was nothing. No furnishings. No windows. No closet. Only white. The walls seamlessly connected to one another. There was no evidence of crease or corners. I stood in its centre staring at the thick white curtains that covered the doorway. I had been dressed in a white, very form-fitting cocktail dress. I wondered how I looked. Not only had I not been allowed to dress, but no mirrors were presented to sate my curiosity of myself. I felt very unappealing with my flesh-pink limbs sticking out of the bottom and sides of the dress. I wore no shoes or socks. I imagined my toes as little twigs protruding from my feet, rooting into the very spot I had been standing in for what seemed like hours.

My body was heavy with exhaustion. It weighed on me like a damp blanket. My shoulders were sore. If someone would have wanted, they may have been able to poke me with a single finger and watch me tip over. I closed my eyes to the thought of that. The thought of falling. Endlessly. Into the nothingness, barely visible brownish amoeba's outlined in a burgundy hue that collided and split from one another over and over. I opened my eyes to escape the abyss of my own wandering mind.

The moment I arrived at this place, my make-up and nail polish had been removed. I was uncomfortable in this state. I felt 'unnatural' without a layer of base and a bit of rouge for my cheeks. Aside from my discomfort with the lack of product, I felt ready. I wanted to transition. A lifetime of torment and abuse had taken its toll on both my mind and body. I needed a reprieve. Thoughts of those horrors started to stand up in line one-by-one.

One of those thoughts stood taller than the rest, in that line. Staring me down from a distance. Reminding me...

August 3, 1995. Laguna California. From what I can recall, I hadn't seen my mother in days. She left me with a so-called friend while she was off finding her next fix. I remember looking out of the living room window seeing children playing with one another or riding their bikes. An elderly couple walked arm-in-arm. The sun shone brightly with the occasional cloud passing in front of it giving the neighbourhood temporary spots of shade. Looking back, it seemed like a quintessential suburban life. Just then, I felt the presence of a man quietly walk up behind me. His shadow seemed to darken the room as he hovered over me. I turned around to see him standing with his hands in his pants pockets. He wore dark blue suit pants held up by black suspenders, going over the shoulders of his white collared shirt. The top two buttons of the shirt were undone. I remember looking down at his shoes, noticing how they shined. Smooth and black.

"Do you like my shoes Abigail?" He asked having observed me taking notice. I looked up to see his face. He was well-kept. Short dark hair combed back. No beard or moustache to speak of. A wide smile with bright white teeth that gave him an inviting aura. I nodded. "Why, thank you! I like yours as well. They are very pretty." He complimented me. I looked down to see my white tap shoes scuffed from wearing them so often. They went along with my white dress that ruffled at the hem, just pass my knees. I recalled having been at church with my mother and aunt a few days prior. I hadn't been home since then. "Thank you..." I whispered. I had no clue who this man was, or whose house it was. I folded my arms and clung to myself.

The man's smile turned into a slight frown as he looked me over. "You look like you've had a rough few days. I think you need a change of clothes and a nice meal. Does that sound good to you?" Once again I nodded my head in agreement as I let out a small, "Yes." "Okay. Wait here. I'm sure my niece has left a few things of hers here. I'll grab it." With that, he smiled and gave me one smooth stroke across the top of my head. He disappeared into the hallway.

I decided to explore the living area a bit, finding my way to a large white sectional sofa and climbing up onto it. My legs stuck straight out in front of me, forcing me to look at my ruined shoes. I thought to myself that my mother would be upset with me if she came to see how I had destroyed my 'good' shoes. I glanced around the living room. It was clean and spacious. A few decorations such as a large plant in a corner and a couple of paintings on the walls, pictures of people in frames on an end table gave it a homely feel. At least in comparison to our apartment, which seemed cramped and dirty. I continued to watch the world outside wishing that I could be there with the other children, running and playing aimlessly.

The man reappeared from the hallway with a white towel slung over his arm and his sleeves rolled up. "Okay Miss Abigail. I found some clothes for you to wear. But first, we have to get you cleaned up before you wear them." He made his way over to the couch and kneeled down in front of me so that he was at my eye level. "Would you like to take a bath so that you can get cleaned up and then have some lunch?" I hadn't realized how hungry I was until that very moment. "I want a pizza." I blurted out in what must have seemed like desperation. He chuckled at my remark, "We can absolutely get some pizza. But first, bath time." He stood up and extended his hand. I took his hand and followed him through the unfamiliar house to a bathroom. It was bright and clean. I looked at the bathtub seeing it was filled just high enough with soapy suds. That made me smile. "Let's get you undressed and into the tub." He placed the towel over his shoulder as he again kneeled down, helping me out of my shoes, placing them behind himself. Next, he unzipped the back of my dress, pulling it off my shoulders and down. I had never been nude in front of anyone but my mother. My level of discomfort shot up as I locked my hands in front of me.

He swiftly but gently picked me up with his hands tucked in my armpits and placed me in the warm tub water. I felt the water overtake my senses, tickling them with much-needed refreshment. Some of the soap splashed onto the bathroom floor. "I'm going to get your clothes cleaned up while you bathe. I'll be back to check on you." I recall not wanting that bath to end. It felt like a safe place. I wanted to shrink down and escape through the drain. But the water would soon turn cold.

***

Two women entered the room, one carrying a large white bowl and the other a large comb along with the same coloured brush. They both wore white straight gowns that were hemmed in gold lace around the wrists and bottoms. Both had very long straightened blonde hair that fell down their waist covering their faces. The two took position behind me.

"Net, derzhat' golovu."

I heard from the right side of my ear as I felt a pair of hands place themselves on both sides of my head and gently position it so that I looked straight forward. The same hands began to gather my stringy black hair and dip it into the large bowl that the second woman was holding. It was not just water alone. It was very sweet smelling. The water being room temperature made it a bit more bearable when the entire bowl was poured over my head. I shivered slightly as it streamed down my face, closing my eyes not so much to avoid the water but to try and decipher the water's content. It smelled of honey, cinnamon, sage and of some sort of flower. The combing of my hair was painful at the start. Frizzy and tangled, the women worked out the knots as gently as they could. In comparison, the brushing felt like gentle foreplay. Long smooth strokes straightening out my hair as it reached down to the middle of my back. The grooming was completed with them pulling my hair into a ponytail and tying it up with a ribbon.

The pair left through the curtains without saying a word. Once again I stood alone. But I knew that it was very nearly time to start. I felt nervous, my fingers clutching to my gown. I could not control my fear of the unknown. I knew that I wanted what was coming, but I had no idea how it would take place. Whatever was expected of me for the transition was unbeknownst to me. Anyone who might have been following my life decisions would find that I had a tendency to jump into things with very little thought. I am reckless. Therein lies my poor decision making.

Once again the curtains were parted, this time by a tall slender woman in a tight-fitting black bridal gown. I wasn't sure of the material of the gown, but it wrapped around her chest and torso as if it were long thick strands of hair trying to cover her exposed body. Her deep red hair flowed down over her shoulders and back almost reaching her waist. Her pale skin looked as smooth as ivory while her long fingernails and lips were painted with a fiery red. Her eyes were devastatingly dark. A black abyss that swirled into a never-ending nothingness. She stepped toward me with an elegance that I had never witnessed before. She stopped just a few inches from me, smiling with what felt like was meant to be a warm smile. She placed her right hand on my left cheek, cupping it. Her touch was dead cold. My muscles tightened up in reaction to the temperature of her skin. I'm sure she noticed the effect she was having on me but chose to ignore it as she pulled my face towards her lips and without moving them spoke, "It is time." My first thought was that delirium had set in from standing in this room for so long. I looked for her to speak again, but she did not. Instead, her eyes spoke to me, implying that I followed her out of the room. She turned and without hesitation, I began to follow. Following close behind her, I could make out the curves of her body. I recall thinking to myself that she was the epitome of what a young girl might consider perfection. She passed through the white curtains, and so did I.

***

The bathwater grew cold and right on que, my newfound caretaker appeared with fresh clothing slung over his left arm. "Okay Miss Abigail, I've got some new clothes for you." He held up a summer dress my size that was covered in pink, yellow and orange floral print. "Are you ready to get out now?" He asked placing the dress on the sink counter. "Yes." I peeped, although if I could have, I would have stayed in that tub as long as humanly possible. He held me with one arm as he reached to grab the folded towel he had left earlier from the top of the toilet tank, then slung it around me like a cape. He put me down to stand on my feet then began drying me off. I felt even more discomfort than before. His movements were slow and methodical. Almost intrusive as he took his time drying me from my feet up to my thighs. My toes dug into the bath rug that covered the floor, as my chin met my right shoulder in attempts to try to hide from what I was feeling. After patting down my hair, he produced a pair of white panties from his back pocket. "Time to get dressed, little one." I lifted one leg at a time as he slid the underwear onto me. Then holding up the dress, I hesitantly held up my arms to allow him to slide the garment down over me. My head popped through the neck of the dress and I was startled to find his face directly in front of mine. "Don't be afraid, little one. I'm going to take very good care of you."

I began to feel sick in the pit of my stomach. The room dissipated to a white nothingness.

STORY FOUR

TURNING OF ABIGAIL FROST- THE CEREMONY

by Shel Henderson

I stepped past the white curtains into a dark walkway. Instead of smooth flooring, my feet encountered what felt like rock and stone. Candles spaced evenly about three feet apart, flickered on the walls to both sides of me very dimly lighting the path ahead. My pale tour guide kept a good lead on me, while in my head her voice spoke to me again, "Keep up child." I began to take longer steps but almost immediately fell off balance causing me to brace myself on the walls. I felt the gravel and loose stone sift through my fingers as I slowly moved along the corridor. I dropped to my knees and vomited. The bile was clear given that I hadn't eaten anything in a day or so. My gut twisted and turned. I began to tear as that memory returned. Returned to sicken me even further.

***

I awoke to find myself in the middle of a queen-sized bed. The sundress I wore moments ago had been removed. Just my panties remained. I attempted to roll over onto my right side but my body went nowhere. I tried to roll the opposite way...to no avail. I went into a paralyzed hysteria. Even in my very short life up until then, I had never felt so much fear and helplessness. I wanted to cry. My eyes darted around the room in a panic. The door to the room flung open startling me. He walked in wearing nothing but a pair of black boxer briefs. He shut the door behind himself then approached the bed. His face was flush and emotionless. His dead eyes focused on me, his prey. He stood at the foot of the bed and stretched his arms behind his head causing a cracking sound. Climbing on to the bed, he hovered over me. That musky smell he permeated lingered and ate away at my senses. He leaned down closer to me kissing me in the middle of my chest. My insides swelled with sickness. His large hand glided over my small body making its way down in between my legs. I was in hell. I had never been touched in such a fashion or encountered someone that made me fear for my life. I wanted my mother. I needed her to come and rescue me from this man...from this monster.

***

Over the years I have done my best to forget. It has never gone away, but I've been able to get through the early stages of my life without thinking about it. Until the night of the ceremony. On that night it flooded back to me vividly. I could not handle the haunting memory of that day any longer. My knees were awash with a burning sensation. I had cuts and scrapes from my fall. I gathered the strength to stand and continue my journey down this cavern corridor.

***

The way widened as I progressed. In the short distance, I could see faint floating lights. This path suddenly opened up into a large ball room-sized area. I found myself among the floating lights. They turned out to be pillar candles held by figures cloaked in black robes. The flooring transitioned abruptly into smooth, cold tiling. The figures stood holding their candles on both sides of the new pathway. I walked slowly in between them, glancing back and forth to try and get a glimpse of a face. But only darkness sat under their hoods.

The woman that had fetched me from the white room stood at the end of the parallel formed lines next to a tall, thick looking figure cloaked in deep red. As I stepped closer to them, that same sweet floral scent I had taken in during the brushing of my hair swirled around me in a light breeze. It was both refreshing and intoxicating. I caught myself smiling to myself. Her words were so sweet while her voice was the most seductive thing that I had ever experienced. Her lips were thin and glossed in a matte black lipstick. Her cheeks were sharp yet her make-up contoured to round them out a bit. Most noticeably, her bright green eyes flared like emeralds being held up to the sun. I was soon to be a puddle sifting through her ring cluttered fingers. I was so coy. My sight looked down into my drink, (that I held with both hands), to avoid looking into her eyes. Thus being trapped there forever.

She was so confident. She ran her fingers through my newly chopped hair slightly brushing my cheek with her palm. "You know that you are in trouble, right?" She asked, her voice, a bit husky for a woman. My eyes shot up to hers in panic, "Wha...what did I do?" I asked in genuine confusion. "You're just so cute!" she replied, with the most egregious of smirks across her lips. I diverted my eyes, looking around the small bar. I remember five other people being there. A trio of guys that looked like they had been there a couple of days straight, an older man seated at the bar that seemed to be contemplating his life with a beer bottle in hand, then someone just leaving.

"Thanks." I tried to be as thankful as possible without showing my embarrassment.

"Where are you from? Here?" She asked, using her hands to flip her fairly long hair to the right side of her face. It was obviously dyed black, with a bronze highlight streaming across the front right. The 'here' she was referring to was Hollywood CA. "No, I'm from Lincoln. I moved here last year."

Was it cool growing up there?" "No...not really..." That was an understatement. "Well, that's shitty. Honestly, I'm not from here either. I was born in bum-drilled Virginia. It. Sucked." Her hatred of her birthplace threw me off. "Is...is that what your town is really called?" I asked stupidly, realizing how stupid my question was. She laughed with a big smile putting her clean white teeth on display. "I'm sorry, that was stupid, I just meant that..." she cut me off before I could explain myself. "It's cool, babe. It's called Belle Haven. It's super small. My parents were meth-heads. Gave me up to my grandmother." She paused for a short moment before picking up her beer from the bar top and taking a huge swig. "I'm sorry that happened to you. My parents weren't around much either. Same situation, drugs." Our newfound commonality made me a little more comfortable. I took a sip of my own drink, a vodka cranberry. "That's the first drink I've seen you take in about ten minutes." she laughed. Once again, my go-to was shyness, but she was ready for it this time. "Hey, gorgeous. You don't have to do that. Relax. We're just two crazy chicks having a good time. Relax, doll."

She reached up to my face and caressed it again. Her palm was warm and reassuring. My shoulders dropped in relaxation as a warming sensation flushed over my body.

***

I stood directly in front of the cloaked figure and waited. Then again, her voice made its way into my head, "You have journeyed far, haven't you, child?" "Yes," I answered out loud. "Do not speak with your lips. Your words can be heard in silence." Although her instructions were clear, I was still confused as to what I should have been doing. "Close your eyes if you must. Focus." I did as told and shut my eyes. "Push away every thought that is not the sound of my voice. Listen. Concentrate. Speak." I followed her instructions step by step until I heard myself engaged in a conversation without having opened my mouth. "I apologize. I didn't mean to be disrespectful." I clasped my hands together in front of me as I did when I was a child. "It is alright, child. The Primus is disturbed by sounds from our vocals. So we are charged to speak with our minds." Her explanation made no sense to me. Why could we not talk out loud? Who was this...Primus? "Step forward. Let the Primus see you." As I took steps forward, that floral scent became strong. I was drawn in. With black-gloved hands, The Primus reached out to me taking my left hand in his right, pulling me closer. Though his face remained in darkness under his hood, I could hear him inhaling through his nose, taking in my scent. He exhaled deeply pushing a cool breath against my face. Strangely I found myself instantly aroused. A warmness filled my chest and my thighs pressed tight together. He placed both of his hands on my shoulders slowly sliding them down my arms until reaching just above my elbows, gripping me tightly.

He leaned down to my face, sniffing long and deep. His cloak rubbed against my face as he sniffed down the right side of my neck. My body warmed further. "You smell of torture and displacement. Your skin reeks of rape and self-hatred. The pain inside you has wrapped itself around your rib cage and does not intend to let go..." his voice was husky and accented. If I could have described it as a smell, it would be as an Amazon jungle. "Give me your discontent. Give me your pain and in return, I will make you a new person. I will make you perfect. No longer will you feel subjugated. Never again will a man harm you." His large hands found their way to the crown of my head. He began to speak in what sounded like a mix of Russian and German. His voice flooded and echoed in my head pulling at my heart. Every agonizing memory I had done my best to forget, came back to me in a reel of real-time horror. My cheeks became soaked in tears of sadness and hopelessness. I was ready to die.

"Give me that life that you wish to leave so badly." His statement caused me to break into a full-on cry. "Are you ready, child?" The woman's voice interceded. "Yes! Yes, please! Kill me!" I sobbed heavily.

With that, The Primus tilted his head back allowing the hood of the cloak to fall from his face and he threw his face into my throat and bit into it. My mouth became stuck open in sheer sharp pain. Her pale hands appeared in my eyesight as I stared up into the darkness of the ceiling of the cavern. She held a clear decanter filled with a thick red substance and began to pour it into my gaped mouth. It was very tart and metallic. As I swallowed, it dawned on me that it was blood. The Primus tightened his jaw around my throat causing me to go limp. I felt as if I was being suspended in mid-air. Quickly, I began to lose consciousness. I welcomed it. I closed my eyes and let the nothingness fall over me.

STORY FIVE

TURNING OF ABIGAIL FROST- THE AWAKENING

by Shel Henderson

Her hair hung down on my face as she leaned down to kiss my lips. They were so soft and warm. Sweat beaded on her face and dripped down onto my own like tropical raindrops falling over a damp jungle. "That...was pretty amazing," Molly exclaimed with a smile on her face. "Don't you agree?" She asked with her eyes closed amidst wrapping her arms underneath and around me. "Yeah, it was," I answered dreamily. I hadn't noticed that my arms were stretched out both sides of me, hanging over the twin-sized bed we occupied. I was absolutely comfortable and relieved at that moment. It was completely unexpected. I had never been with another girl to this capacity.

***

I looked around me to find that I was sitting in a very shallow grave. It couldn't have been more than a foot deep. My legs were covered in damp dirt. I inspected myself and saw that my pink skin was now porcelain white. While the white dress I wore had been removed, I now wore a red one in the same styling in its place. I smiled to myself. Not because I liked what I was adorned in, but because I felt different...rejuvenated...new. "Rise. My daughter. "The voice of The Primus snapped me out of my self-concern. His robe had been exchanged for a black suit. He wore a black silk shirt with no tie, the top two buttons undone. Even from where I sat I could tell that he was in an impeccable shape. His hand was outstretched to me, inviting me to join him. To his right stood the slender redhead woman from before. Still, in her black ball gown, her hands were joined behind her back. She came across absolutely regal and full of confidence. I began to bend my knees causing the dirt in my lap to part and fall to the sides of my legs. I stood up and started walking towards the two. The moon was full and bluish in the distance behind them. My senses were alive and almost at full throttle. Everything was amplified. I could smell bark and foliage of a nearby forest as well as hear the scuttles and squeaks of small animals that it housed as if they were running right in front of me. I drew close and The Primus turned his hand palm down. Without thought or instruction, I lowered myself to both my knees, and taking his hand with both of mine, kissed it. I was grateful.

***

Molly sat on the edge of the bed, pulling her grey t-shirt over her and down her torso. I glanced in time enough to see a glimpse of the tattoo on her back. I made out what looked like a sneering goat with curved elongated horns. My attention was drawn to my nakedness causing me to slowly pull the bedspread up to my chest, covering myself. "Are you cold?" she asked while slipping on her black. "I'm fine...just..." I couldn't think of an excuse that made sense. "Just embarrassed all of a sudden? No...well...I don't know. I guess it was just a reaction. I suppose..." The embarrassment set in and I began to stumble over my thoughts. Mentally scolding myself for not being more confident. "Listen, girly. You have to start living your life before you die. We had a good time tonight. You have nothing to be ashamed of or embarrassed about. Everything is good." And once more, she smiled her smile at me. That made everything okay. It made me okay. I placed my left hand to her right cheek and prompted her to lean towards me for a kiss. She did so, setting my lips and nerves afire. "Hey, do you want to meet my family?" Molly asked, throwing me absolutely off guard. "Your family? I thought that you didn't like your family?" "Well, they aren't my blood relatives. Even though they kind of are. It's a whole thing, you have to meet them to find out. So do you want to?" Her eyes were wide, intense with anticipation. "Sure, Molly. I'll go." She smiled.

***

The Primus' eyes were a steely combination of every colour. I wasn't sure how that was possible, but each time they were caught in the moonlight, it was almost like seeing a rainbow in a rain puddle. His skin was a faded bronze. Much like a statue sculpted in ancient Greece that had been battered by centuries of winter. His face was the very epitome of beauty. Not just handsome, but beauty. I suppose perfection would be a better term to use. I thought to myself that his face must have been chiseled very carefully by hand. "Not quite." I was startled by the response to my thoughts. My eyes shot over to The Primus' lady companion. There she stood, ever regal. "Our Lord was not created by the hands of the common man. He has a much more 'definitive' beginning. You shall learn of that soon enough. Come, Lady Abigail, it is time that your purpose is explained."

"I am Catalina. I am The Primus' 'First'. It is my charge to guide you through the first steps of your transition, as well as prepare you for this life. Is that understood?" "Yes, I understand," I replied, finding more confidence in my voice than I had ever had in the entirety of my life. "Good. This way, child." Catalina stretched her hand in front of us, motioning to a waiting vehicle ahead. It was bone white and elongated, but not quite a limo. We reached the car and Catalina pulled the handle of the backdoor, opening it in front of me. My sense of smell was immediately tackled by a heavy scent of blood. It smelled musky yet barely sweet. My heart began to race with excitement. My thighs began to warm with want. An intense almost uncontrollable hunger washed over me. "Look inside," Catalina instructed.

A man sat in the car seat that faced the opposite way. His shirt was soaked with what I assumed was his own blood. There he sat silently. Lifelessly. But I could tell that he was alive. From where I stood, a few couples of feet away, I could hear his heart beating. "Sit next to him." I did as told. Catalina sat across from me, while The Primus entered the car from the other side, sitting across from their bleeding guest. "Do you recognize this man?" Catalina asked. I looked the man over. Nothing in particular about him revealed his identity to me. "No, I don't," I answered casually. Catalina looked at The Primus, he only nodded at her before she returned her sights to me. "Take a closer look...a deeper look." I looked him up and down again. He was middle-aged. Well-built. Greyish short hair that was combed back. His now red button-up shirt, once white, was neatly tucked into his black suit pants. But his shoes...his shoes were what caught my attention.

"Do you like my shoes, Abigail?"

They were smooth and glossy. Like holy relics. My eyes shot back up to his face. His head was turned away from me slumped on his right shoulder. I grabbed him by his jaw and turned his head to me. "I like yours as well. They are very pretty..." His voice addressed me from all of those years ago. The warmth in my thighs had moved up and into my chest. Rage was forming. His face was drained of colour and fatigue worn. “Wake up...” I commanded. “What's your name?” His eyes barely fluttered as he mumbled something unintelligible. “His name is Adam Scott. Born in Youngstown Ohio, but has resided in Laguna California for the past 20 years or so. His hobbies are tennis, model aeroplane building and raping of very young girls. This is Lord Starets' gift to you, child. A token of appreciation for your dedication to this coven. You are very important to us. We treat our loved ones as such. Now...feed.”

I could not recall the last time that I had been given a gift so worthwhile. Just as anyone else in life, it has always been trivial, “Well here's some makeup or a sweater for your birthday.” This gift was the only thing that I had ever truly wanted. But I had not realized it until this very moment. So I fed.

I leaned back in the seat, calm and satisfied. The heat in my chest had been subdued to a cooling state. My thoughts were blank. I looked across to my superiors, they both gave me approving grins.

***

Epilogue: The Red

My grip on his jaw tightened. He made a small whimper from the pressure of it. Again, I asked, “What's your name?” A gargled “I” climbed out of his throat. I realized that my hold was partially obstructing his airway. I squeezed tighter. The bones of his jaw snapped under my fingers like brittle plastic. I watched his eyes open wider as his pupils dilated. I've often wondered what my eyes conveyed to him. I've always felt assured that they did not display pain or hurt. I had given him my emotions for so many years. Locked up inside the little girl that had been so maliciously violated. No, the time for pain was over. At least for me.

My nose was battered by the smell of fear. It was absolutely intoxicating. This was the smell of anticipation. Of the unknown of what horror was about to fall upon him. Endorphins. Epinephrine. I was swimming in it; as he was soaked in it.

Still holding on to his crumbled jaw, I lunged toward him with my own mouth open. Biting into the left side of his neck effortlessly, his blood squirted into my waiting throat in quick short bursts. My thighs were pulsating. I clutched to the back of Adam's head to keep him from adjusting in either direction. My fingernails dug into his skull, beginning to rake into the thin layer of membrane of his skin. The flow of blood could not come quickly enough. And it didn't. In efforts to increase the draining, I started to chew at his neck. I slung my body on top of his, straddling his lap, not releasing my hold. Inadvertently rolling my hips. My chewing grew more intense. At first, the muscles were stiff. As a scalene muscle would be if a man were in immediate shock. I was sure that I was biting into the posterior. As I chewed, the meat became softened and became more pliable. Small chunks of muscle rolled onto my tongue and between my teeth. My tongue felt engorged. I gnawed. I gnashed. And for all intents and purposes; I came...

Taking one last bite, I pulled away from him to gather myself, still chewing the chunks of flesh I had taken. I admired the damage that I had done to his face and neck. Satisfied that although I wasn't his first, or his last victim, I was the last thing that he saw and felt. I was able to take back what so many other little girls could not. I took back his life.

STORY SIX

PAIN

by Snehal Agarwal

Firecrackers shone brightly in the sky as the ceremony came to an end. The exhausted couple were finishing up the last rituals and a car for their departure was already at the gate of the venue. The family and friends of the beautiful bride were in tears as she was about to bid adieu to them. The air was thick with sadness and a big fat Indian arranged wedding was coming to an end.

The bride was unable to accept the fact that tonight she would not be sleeping in her own cozy bed but with a stranger whom she met only a few months back. “You will eventually fall in love with him completely, he is such a sweet guy,” she consoled herself as they proceeded towards the exit.

The wedding zest was now overpowered by loud sobs and wails of her relatives. Her now-husband walked ahead of her while she trailed him. It felt as if he was a little too eager to go back home, making her shudder at the thought of what awaits for her in the future. To seek some comfort, her gaze met her father's eyes and she broke down on seeing him cry uncontrollably. This man, who was her strongest pillar, looked so pale. He hugged his departing daughter tightly and whispered, "Remember papa loves you a lot!".

Her childhood days flashed in front of her eyes as they embraced each other. From the days when he used to hug her every night before bed to make sure she was at home in time for bed, when did she grow up enough to get married? From holding her hand and travelling around the world with her, to holding her hand only to give it away to an unknown man, what changed? Her heart pounded as she recalled those days. "Don't worry Divya, Arjun has promised to protect and love you more than papa," she reminded herself as she moved behind her husband.

Her mother, weeping in a corner, finally mustered the courage to rush towards Divya and engulf her. Broken sentences of loving forever were spoken amidst the incessant tears. Divya recalled the days when her mom used to dress her up for school and compared how different it felt when she dressed her up today for her wedding. Her makeup smeared across her face because of the constant tears as the goodbyes continued.

Finally, at the exit, they said their last goodbyes and got into the car. Arjun shuffled in his seat to extract a handkerchief to wipe his wife's tears. "You know you will meet your family again, soon," he said as he caressed her tear-stained face. She nodded. "Will Arjun love me as he promised? Will I be able to adjust with his family? What if I can't do something they are expecting me to do?" Multiple questions haunted her and a frown appeared on her face.

They reached Arjun's house soon and his parents were already waiting for their welcome. They made her feel at home and retired to their own room, giving the newlyweds their privacy. Arjun's eyes danced with excitement as she settled in her new room. Divya knew what was expected of her on the wedding night but was she ready to do anything with Arjun? But again, was there any option? She gulped.

She reluctantly dressed up for the night, not wanting to defy an Indian woman's duty to make her husband happy on their wedding night and on every night after it, whenever her husband felt like it. She just hoped for it to be beautiful, full of love and excitement.

Arjun, already in bed, asked her to join him. She hesitantly obeyed. His hands stroked her hair and then moved towards her neck. She closed her eyes, his soft skin brushed her gently, making her feel weak in her knees. Heat radiated from his hands and she was caving into his touch. He leaned in closer, hovering over her face. His warm breath, tickling her.

"Aaghhh!", she choked suddenly. The realization struck her when she was unable to breathe, his strong hands were around her neck, pressing it hard. Her arms flailed as she tried to escape his painful grasp. Her vision blurred within moments and she kicked her legs and clawed at him to let her go. His laughter reached her ears faintly before she gave up. That's when he released his grip. Gasping for air, she moved away from him frantically and looked at her husband with fear and disgust.

"I'm sorry, are you alright? It will never happen again," he quickly asked, his voice laced with concern. Not understanding what just happened, she stared blankly at him. He pulled her softly, apologizing and holding her close. After making her feel better, he got on top of her. His eerie eyes shone brighter. He looked at her calmly before he slapped her right across her face. She shrieked in immense pain and his laughter again echoed in the room.

Her husband derived pleasure by inflicting pain. How will she survive this?

STORY SEVEN

CHEATING

by Dr. Anuraag Awasthi

My husband is cheating on me," Saumya confided in Dr. Pooja, her psychotherapist. It had taken her a lot of courage to be able to face this truth and decide to deal with it.

Saumya was a very beautiful, tall, 32-year-old woman. But as her friends would say, she did not look a day more than a 25-year-old. From a very young age, she had been regularly practicing yoga which not only resulted in a fit body but also brought a glow on her face. She had a very athletic build, long curly hair, and was very fond of dressing up. Professionally, she was an interior decorator and had to visit rich clients. So, her fashionable dress sense added to her self-confidence.

But, right now, sitting in front of Dr. Pooja, her confidence appeared shaken. She looked a pale shadow of herself. Dr. Pooja offered her a glass of water to calm her nerves. Both kept quiet for some time. Eventually, the psychotherapist broke the ice – "How are you feeling now? If it is ok with you, could you remove your goggles?"

"Oh, sure", Saumya removed her shades, and also removed the stole covering her head.

In our country, there is a stigma attached to mental health issues. Though some celebrities have come out in the open about their fights with depression, and there is a growing acceptance of this as any other illness, people still have privacy concerns. They do not want others to know that they are seeking professional help. It helped that Dr. Pooja's clinic was in a remote part of the city. To be extra cautious, Saumya had put on dark glasses and covered her head with a stole, before entering her clinic.

Dr. Pooja smiled at her – a very pleasant, empathetic, professional smile. A gold medalist in her college, she had 15 years of experience and was widely regarded for her professional competence. She explained the whole process of counselling, assuring her complete confidentiality. Patience is a key requirement in counselling, and Pooja had it in abundance. Before beginning her investigation, she requested Saumya to tell her about her life, education, family, friends, nature of the problem, any existing medication etc. Saumya's antenna was instantly up. Should she tell everything correctly? What if her identity gets revealed? She decided to tell all the facts correctly but changed her own name.

"I am Avika, a professionally trained interior decorator. I have a small family - my husband, our 7-year-old son, and my mother-in-law. My husband is in a high-profile corporate job and earns very well. My son is studying in a decent school, I am also earning – so from that angle, we could be considered a model, happy family. But a few months back I noticed that my husband's behaviour had changed. He started returning late from office, would even go out on weekends on some pretext, and his phone would always come engaged. He stopped taking interest in house responsibilities. When I confronted him, he flatly refused. I am 100% sure he is seeing someone. Our marital relations have broken down. We have regular fights between us. I am depressed. My husband is cheating on me," she blabbered on.

Dr. Pooja did not react. She kept a quarter-smile on, nodding indulgently in between. During her long career as a practicing psychotherapist, she had come across all sorts of cases, and nothing surprised her anymore. There had been cases of depression, anxiety, trauma, addictions, fetish etc. For the last few years, however, the cases of marital infidelity and breakups leading to depression and suicidal thoughts had increased. It was, perhaps, a reflection on the changing morals and values in society.

By now Saumya had regained her composure, having the load off her chest. For the rest of the session, Saumya spoke more about her cold married life, her own profession, her husband's drinking habits, lack of warmth in the relationship etc. and how she was on the verge of a breakdown due to her husband's philandering ways. These were a normal part of modern life, Pooja thought. After a few years of married life, partners do drift apart. She herself was having such issues in her life, but as a psychologist, she understood that these were 'normal'. They decided to meet every week for more hourly sessions.

She was given some mindfulness exercises to do, to note down her own emotions at various points of time, the triggers, the body reactions etc. With each session, Saumya opened a little more. Her body language had begun to change. She spoke more assertively. But to Pooja, something seemed amiss. She just couldn't place it. Finally, in the fourth session, Saumya exploded a bombshell. She entered Pooja's cabin with a bang.

“I want to teach him a lesson. I will not leave him like this. He has used me.” She fumed.

“Used you? How? He is your husband,” Pooja asked.

“I am not talking about him. I am talking about my boyfriend. He has used me.” Saumya was furious, her face red with anger.

OMG. Pooja was both startled and amused at the same time. Keeping a straight face, she asked her to tell more.

Saumya had gathered her breath by now. Her face reflected a strange resolve. She continued - “The place where I am working as a designer, he is one of the senior managers. I joined them about a year back. Since we had to go out for client meetings, we used to often travel together. We became quite friendly and also started meeting outside office hours. One day when we were alone in the office, he kissed me. When I resisted, he forced himself on me. I was taken aback by the sudden turn of events, but couldn’t react. Then it happened a few more times, and I sort of started liking it. With my husband, I had never had such passionate relations. It was intoxicating. He told me that he was also not happy in his marriage, and promised that he would divorce his wife and marry me.”

“And what about your husband? And your boyfriend’s wife? Do they have any idea?”

“Oh, his wife is a bitch, always fighting with him. That is why he got interested in me. And my husband is a very nice man. He loves me a lot, but it is not about him. It’s about my boyfriend. Last month I discovered that I had become pregnant with him. When I broke the news to him and asked about our promised marriage, he took a complete U-turn. He started ignoring me. And now he is asking me to abort the child and get lost. He has disowned me.”

Pooja had seen many such cases of infidelity, but this was unique. Saumya had come to her for treatment of depression, as she claimed. She had told stories about her husband's infidelity and how it had broken her. And now after four sessions, that story turns out fake. She wasn't interested in talking about her husband anymore. No one can guess what goes inside a woman's mind, Pooja thought.

"Ok, so what do you want now?" she asked. "Do you want to abort, seek family counselling, or marry him... what is your plan?"

"I want to teach him a lesson he will remember for life. I will not abort the child. I told him that I was willing to divorce my husband and marry him, and he had also been promising the same. But today he called me a woman of loose character. He says I was an equal partner in all this, and in fact, I had enticed him. I feel so used. How dare he treat me like this, how dare he call me characterless? I will screw his life. He doesn't know who I am. I will ruin his marriage." Saumya was seething with anger.

"But how will you prove that he is the father of your child? How can you force him to marry you?" Pooja naively asked.

"Oh, don't you worry. I have his messages and promises to marry me in my phone as evidence. I also have selfies with him in bed in compromising positions. Let him deny these and I will show these messages and pics to his wife and post them on social media. If he can play a game with me, I can also pay him back in the same coin. He has called me characterless, now I will show him who is characterless. I will force that bastard to divorce his wife and marry me."

Saumya was on her own trip. As if to prove her case to Pooja, she opened her phone's message box and showed a few of those messages to her. Pooja didn't want to see them but was caught in an awkward position. As she read a few of those explicit messages, her ears became red with embarrassment, her breath raced. How shameless, she thought.

"Let me also show you our pictures. You will be shocked to know how close we were." Saumya seemed excited about seeing the blush on Pooja's face.

Before Pooja could say anything, Saumya opened the picture gallery and slowly started scrolling the images of their private moments. Pooja was cornered and had no choice than to look at them. As each image floated in front of her eyes, they kept getting wider and wider. Her body started trembling, her throat parched, even as her eyes remained fixated on the mobile screen. She picked up the glass of water lying on the table and gulped it in one go.

'See, I told you, you will be shocked. We did all this, and now this as.h.le is refusing marriage. I will make his life hell. I will post it on social media, I will show it to his wife. Let me see how she reacts." Saumya was lost in her own thoughts. Suddenly she noticed that Pooja's face had turned pale. She had sunk in her seat with drops of sweat visible on her forehead, even in that AC environment.

"What happened? Are you ok? Do you know him?"

With great effort, in a very weak voice, words came out of Pooja's dry mouth – "He is my husband."

Saumya put the phone back in her bag, and took out a visiting card. Then bending forward, she brought her face right in front of Pooja's face, and with an evil smile, whispered in her ear –

"Yes... I know."

Tears streamed down Pooja's face.

Saumya got up from her seat and began to leave. Then she suddenly turned around and said "Oh, by the way, here is a card of a divorce lawyer. You will need it."

STORY EIGHT

UNFAITHFUL

by Kriti Medirатta

Throwing things here and there, Trisha was walking around in frustration, fed up with all the sarcasm she had to listen to at her work because of her flirty husband. Her so-called friend Riya had just called her to prove the point of how good a husband she has whereas Trisha doesn't. She threw the phone and sat on the sofa and shouted loudly, "I am really a fool who married this stupid guy because of his sweet words. I won't let this happen again! I am not going to fall for his sweet words and charm again. Now I will prove to him what Trisha Gupta, Oh! no no, what Trisha Arora can do and how miserable I can make his life."

She picked up her phone and dialled her best friend Pooja. The plan was made and the details were decided, it only had to be executed. Now that anger had vanished, she smiled cunningly and said to nobody in particular, "Now no one can save you, my darling husband Devesh."

As planned by the two friends, Trisha bought surveillance cameras and fixed one in each room and one outside the house too. For the next phase of the plan, she told Devesh that she would be spending the night at her friend's place but in reality, her plan was to book into a hotel room and watch his activities through her laptop. Devesh was completely unaware of his wife's plans since there was nothing unusual about Trisha going to her friend's place.

When the night finally approached, Trisha set up three laptops and watched the live feed of her own house from the hotel room she was staying at. After waiting for many restless hours, she finally saw something that came both as a shock and confirmation that her husband was indeed cheating on her. Devesh and a beautiful young girl were sitting together on their sofa and they looked very comfortable around each other. Even though they weren't kissing each other, Trisha's instinct told her to believe the worst - that her husband was adulterous.

Staring with a fixed eye on the laptop, seeing those two together, she was breaking down emotionally but not a single tear came out. She always believed herself to be a strong woman who controlled things around her rather than letting the society control her. When her father had died 20 years ago, she fought back against all odds and took the responsibility of her mother on herself. Trisha was a brave girl with high morals in life. The accident in which her father died did affect her emotionally, but she never let it reflect on her face. She showed the world how to survive a loss.

She zoomed in on the woman's face and tried to recall where she had seen her before. That's when the name hit her – Mia, yes that's who this woman was. The homewrecker! Mia was Devesh's personal assistant who had joined his office around four months ago. Whenever she would visit her husband's office, Mia would be hovering around with her annoying aura that would make Trisha irritated and uncomfortable.

"Has Devesh been cheating on me from the past four months? Was I just too stupid to realize it sooner? I have to know all the secrets he has been hiding from me!" she thought bitterly. It was her sole mission now.

Next day, she packed her stuff, rang up Pooja and visited her house with yet another plan. She knew she had to get to the bottom of this and this was just the start. According to the plan, they had also invited Samarth, a common friend of the couple to Pooja's house. Unsuspecting, he reached right on time and the trio had a hearty breakfast. After a while silence engulfed the room and Trisha knew it was time to make Samarth blurt out the truth.

She asked him in a calm, yet threatening voice, one that would send shivers down your spine. "Being my husband's best friend, you are the perfect person to ask about his whereabouts? Isn't it?" Samarth nodded in a 'yes', he was dazed. After listening to the seriousness in Trisha's voice, he was busy anticipating what was coming next.

Trisha got up from her seat and walked around the room gesticulating and muttering to herself. After contemplating the situation for a minute, she finally spoke with a hint of anger in her voice, "So tell me Samarth, what is going on between my husband and his assistant? Is he cheating on me?"

Samarth's prediction was right, he knew this question was bound to come his way sooner or later. He replied in his best convincing tone. "I am sure nothing is happening between them. Yes, they have become very close friends recently. But that's what they are, workplace friends."

Trisha quickly took the knife kept with fruits and pointed it toward Samarth and shouted, "Better tell me the truth otherwise you know no one is more dangerous than a woman who is cheated on."

Samarth knew he had to confess now. "Devesh had taken her to some hotels a few times and he used to pay with my debit card so that you don't get to know. Now I don't know what they did inside the room and I never asked him. But it's obvious? Isn't it?" Samarth said directly without beating around the bush.

She sunk low on the sofa, cupped her face in both her palms and sat dejected. "Thank you both for being here but I need some time alone, so please leave." Trisha was hurt by the betrayal but had no wish to confront anyone or hold on to false hopes of everything to be fine again. She decided that the best thing for her to do was to move on.

Pooja gladly took her in her home and helped her look for jobs. Trisha wanted to be independent now and have money to pay rent to her best friend and also start a new life for herself. Two months went by and she never once went back to her former home, neither responded to any of Devesh's calls. The confused man still tried figuring out what went wrong given that Trisha never confronted him with the truth she had found out about him.

She knew she should have talked to Devesh, cleared out the air with him, not trusted Samarth completely because after all, she had very vague proof about the cheating. But in her heart, she knew she hated confrontations and didn't want to feel weak before Devesh. She went along with accepting the betrayal. She carried on with her low-salaried, under-paying job and kept on looking for better opportunities.

Life went on. Once on a break from work, Trisha was sitting in a coffee shop when she saw Mia was coming towards her table.

"Can I sit here? There are no other empty seats around," she politely asked.

"Sure," Trisha replied. They both exchanged pleasantries and started to talk. They even exchanged numbers. Trisha had no anger against her but was rather kind towards her, just like she would treat any other stranger.

A week passed by since their encounter when they bumped into each other again, same time, same place.

Trisha had earlier mentioned to Mia that she was looking for a better job. Out of the blue, Mia offered Trisha a job. She expounded on the details of the job to her. It was a role of a verifier. The verifier has to seek for corroborations through both legal and illegal ways. The legal ways included the basic document checking but the illegal ways composed of unlicensed stalking and talking to people in disguise. The concealing nature of the job gave her chills of excitement and adventure. The pay was significantly higher, this job can help her move out of Pooja's home. She had already started day-dreaming about her sumptuous house.

The next day, Trisha reached the place Mia had called her to. It was an abandoned building; Trisha could already feel the thrill and the adrenaline rush. She thought of this opportunity in the most optimistic way. The only stumbling block between her and the job was a senior's approval.

Submitting her fingerprints made her come back to reality. She was meticulously listening to all the instructions by Mia and following her like a lost puppy. They reached the senior's room and Mia left the astonished Trisha there. After collecting her thoughts, Trisha knocked and entered the room. When she saw the person sitting in the 'senior's' chair, she was dumbstruck. Her excitement and joy were replaced by questions, fear and panic. She had never in a million years imagined the possibility of what was happening. Sitting there in front of her, Pooja, her childhood friend looked at her with a perfect poker face. She extended her hand toward Trisha and after realizing what she meant, Trisha handed her the form. Pooja stamped "Rejected" on her form.

Both of them didn't utter a word. The silence and tension in the air were strong enough to cut metal. Trisha took her form and stormed out of the room.

After coming home, Trisha noticed that Pooja didn't return yet. She was getting very impatient every minute. She needed answers. Fortuitously, she found Pooja's diary lying on the corner showpiece rack, and in that split second of the decision, she decided to read it. All the pages were of Pooja's daily life all what Trisha already knew about. She kept flipping the pages when something written in the diary caught her eye.

"I love you Samarth. I love you. And you, you never look back at me with that love. We work together but you never ask me on a date. When you told me that you love Trisha I was shocked and hurt. But still, I tried to get her out of her marriage only for you my darling. Though THE BOSS was not ready, I took the risk only for you. I love you so much."

She stood stunned and read the entry again and again. It took her a while to process the information. But when she finally came to her senses, she knew she had to investigate more. She won't make the same mistake twice. She wanted to know the truth, she won't 'let go' this time.

She was wandering aimlessly around the house, thinking of some way to solve this weird mystery. Eventually, she got the idea to call one of her college friends who she knew was now a detective. It was important for the plan that Trisha hide behind the veil of normal behavior. Any kind of inkling can alert Pooja more.

Three days had passed and both of them were avoiding each other. Trisha's detective friend called her and told that both Mia and Samarth have confidential and sealed files. She had found that both Pooja and Samarth's call list had a jillion of phone calls from Trisha's mother.

Trisha never thought that her mother would be involved in this puzzle. She decided to go and confront her mother because getting answers from her would be easier than getting answers from Pooja or Samarth. Trisha was at a point where weird things were happening around her but the impossible and astonishing thing happened when she entered her house.

Her 'supposedly dead' father was standing beside her mother, very much alive. Trisha couldn't believe her eyes. It felt like she was in a dream. Then her mother started unravelling the truth. Pooja, Samarth, and Mia work for them and that the accident was fake. It was done to show the world that her father was dead. In reality, Trisha's father was the head mafia of the largest mafia group of the country. As if this wasn't quite enough, they told her that Devesh was his company's CEO but he was also working as a government's secret agent. That's why her mother insisted that she should marry Devesh. She was married to him for information and when she didn't help much in getting any, they roped in Mia to do the job. Even Pooja and Samarth were a part of the plan.

She listened to everything quietly, still trying to wrap her head around the truth of her existence. It hurt her to believe how her own loved ones had used her as a puppet, how their lies had ruined her life. She knew nothing could be the same ever but there was still one last thing for her left to do. She quietly slipped from there and went to Devesh to tell him everything and get her parents arrested.

STORY NINE

ASPIRATIONS, DREAMS & EVILDOERS

by Adyasha Mishra

It was a beautiful day in a small town near Ranchi. Anita woke up rubbing her eyes, still dazed from her slumber sleep. The sun shone brightly outside her wooden window carved with flowers while the birds chirped away happily. She gave out a big yawn, flipped her hair and turned towards the mirror. Then she smiled brightly.

Meet Anita Dungroo, a 17-year-old high-school student who dreamt of becoming a successful model someday. Her mind spilled with ideas about almost everything. Anyone who met her would be mesmerized by her beauty and impressed by her confident, enthusiastic personality. Every morning, she made it a routine to practice her walk in front of her full-length mirror and perfect it each time. Amidst all this, she eagerly waited for her class 12th to get over.

Then she would get to give wings to her dreams by flying to the big city and fulfill her aspirations of becoming a top-notch model. She had it all planned out and would often day dream about the big day.

Anita's mother, Rajnandini Dungroo was a very sweet person, modern, open-minded and a highly educated woman. After her marriage, she had left her career behind to look after the needs of her new family. Her absent father, Rajiv Dungroo was a successful entrepreneur, an alcoholic and a heartless individual who had abandoned his family two years ago to move in with his girlfriend in Kolkata. Before bidding them goodbye, he had assured them of his constant financial support as a way to cover up for his infidelity and abandonment. However, Anita's mother would hear none of it. If he wanted to leave, he would have to leave them fully. She wanted no trace of his presence in their lives, leave alone seeking financial help. She looked for jobs and soon enough got accepted as a History lecturer in a prestigious university owing to her impressive educational background.

Today was an ordinary day as well. She got up, put on her heels and practiced her walk quickly, brushed her teeth, took a bath, ate breakfast and took a while getting ready for school. She never hesitated to give a nice stroke to her eyes with kajal and eyeliner. She loved to look different.

"Come fast, beta!" her mother shouted.

"Coming, Maa!" Anita replied.

Closing the lid of her kajal pencil, she ran to the drawing-room where her mother was waiting for her, holding her tiffin in one hand and her school bag in another. She was wearing a gorgeous green-red saree. She loved wearing beautiful outfits to her work. Anita took the bag from her mother's hand and slowly glided the kajal into her bag's front pocket. Rajnandini locked the main door and both of them jogged to their society's gate as they were running late. Seeing the bus arrive, they increased their speed and like any other typical Indian mother, she reminded Anita to finish her tiffin. After making sure her daughter was seated in the bus, Rajnandini kept waving her hands until the bus turned into the corner and vanished from her sight. She smiled, took out her perfumed handkerchief from her purse and wiped out the sweat from her forehead. She walked back inside the society to get her scooter. It took merely 7 minutes for her to reach the University, provided there was moderate traffic.

On the other hand, Anita's school wasn't near. It was 25 kilometres away. She always chose the window seat so that the breeze would blow into her hair while she look outside and daydream about her future. Her dreams were huge. She used to carry a fashion magazine with her and look at all the exciting outfits and imagine how she would look on the ramp someday. She felt blessed and lucky because her mother believed in her and supported her dreams.

The days passed by quickly. Each day felt like a year to Anita as she couldn't wait to step into her glamour world. At last, it was the final board exams which made her happy and excited. She returned home with the widest smile on her face. She never cared about how her exams went. She was a below-average student who was happy and satisfied if the results came between 60%- 65%. Her mother rang up her younger sister in Mumbai to inform her that Anita would be reaching there in a few days. Rajnandini's sister, Shikha and her husband, Dhruv lived in a 2 BHK flat in Mumbai's Andheri East. They were newly married and didn't have any kids yet so they were more than happy to take Anita in. Everything went smoothly. Rajnandini booked the train ticket for Anita and they started packing all the essentials. Anita made sure to pack all the attractive outfits she had collected over these years. Both of them were extremely excited. Anita was far matured for her age. She was self- assured that she would handle everything alone. Meanwhile, she collected all the information about modelling agencies and commercial castings in Mumbai.

6th May, finally the day arrived. Anita woke up before her alarm rang. She was too electrified that morning. She got ready quickly. Her mother booked a cab for the Ranchi railway station and they soon left the house. Waiting at the platform, Anita said, "I'll miss you, Maa". Her mother almost had a tear in her eye, but she didn't want the situation to turn emotional and nervous for both of them. "I'll miss you too, sweetheart. But you'll be fine. Uncle and aunt will take good care of you," she replied.

The train arrived on time at 10:30 am and both of them got inside to find her seat. Rajnandini put the luggage beneath Anita's seat and gave a kiss on her forehead before leaving her to venture the world out alone for the first time. She softly said, "Bye beta, take care." Anita was too excited and tough to get emotional even for one second. She watched her mother step down the train and both of them waved a final goodbye to each other. The train slowly departed. Now alone, Anita sat back and started to imagine all the things she would do once she reached the city. After a long wait of 35 hours, she finally reached the City of dreams: MUMBAI. Her uncle and aunt were already present at the platform to receive her. They drove her to their house. It was already 11:00 p.m. Her aunt had cooked some Schezwan noodles and Manchurian for Anita. She was tired but very happy to be there. Before she could fall asleep, she made sure to place a video call to her mother.

The next morning turned out to be the most exciting and most awaited morning for Anita. She had a list of seven modeling agencies to approach that day. She gave the auditions and people were impressed by her confidence and the way she spoke. Not just she was pretty, she was tall and carried a beautiful smile and she literally would gather all the attention whenever she entered any hall or a stage. She was totally exhausted after giving five auditions, but she didn't give up. She re-energized herself and gave the remaining two auditions with the same enthusiasm. Days passed, she gave more than 80 auditions and waited for their confirmation calls.

One morning, she received a call from an agency. She was extremely joyful and went to meet the casting director of that agency.

"May I come in, sir," she pleasantly asked.

"Oh yes, dear. Please have a seat." A young man with thick glasses replied. "You're extremely beautiful and talented." He said.

"Thank you sir," she blushed and replied. He rose from his chair and came near Anita. He planted his right hand on Anita's left thigh and said, "You will be a supermodel very soon." The gesture made her extremely nervous. She gave a fake smile to him. Although she was just 17, she knew the difference between good touch and bad touch. She hesitated a little and asked, "Sir, may I know where's the washroom?" He instructed her verbally and finally, Anita got a chance to flee. She was very disturbed but decided not to say anything about this. For some days, she remained indoors and waited for more calls.

Then one Sunday morning at 9:30 am, she received a call from Bikram who happened to be her uncle's friend. She excitedly ran to her uncle to inform him about the news.

Her uncle replied, "Oh my God, that's great. I have known him for the past 9 years now. Come, I'll take you to him." Both of them reached the production house. Bikram shook hands with them and asked them to have a seat. Anita witnessed that her uncle and Bikram were talking something through gestures and expressions. This seemed fishy to her. Bikram asked his servant to bring juice for both of them. Anita drank the juice, sip by sip. After a few moments, she experienced a severe headache and fell unconscious.

***

Her eyes opened in the evening. It was approximately 6:30 pm. She saw herself lying on the bed and realised that the T-shirt she wore was reversed. She was shocked. She heard some noise coming from outside. When she put her feet on the floor, her whole body ached badly. She was not able to walk properly. She opened the door slightly and found her uncle and Bikram laughing and gossiping about the fun Bikram had with Anita while she was unconscious. She was dismayed. Dhruv was a father-figure to her and experiencing all this, just broke her to the core. She decided to go to them and act normally as if she didn't know what all happened. She went near them and gave a slight smile. Dhruv said, "Oh, come beta. You were not feeling well so we let you sleep."

Anita asked, "Can we go home?"

"Oh yes, of course. Your aunt must be waiting for us," Dhruv replied.

The confident girl who had so many dreams, now broke into pieces. All she wanted now was to return to her mother's lap. After reaching her aunt's flat, she called her mother and asked her to book the train ticket for her return. Her mother was confused but happy as well. Why not, she was going to meet her daughter after a huge gap of 45 days. She informed her uncle and aunt that she was missing her mom very much and assured that she would be back in 10 days. She could see the cunning smile on her uncle's face which disturbed her even more.

She reached Ranchi and hugged her mother tightly the second she stepped down the train. She remained quiet for a very long time. Days passed but she never opened up. She could see her dreams shattering in front of her. She finally decided to help and give modeling classes to the little girls of her town who had big dreams. She started giving classes at her place. With her mother's help, she renovated her drawing room so that the students could get a bigger space to learn. It took time for her to settle, but finally, she was happy and loved her work.

***

Anita was unlucky to get all the monsters in her career's initial stage. She couldn't become a top model but she made sure that every girl could dream about anything they wanted to become. You'll find monsters and mean people in every field you step in. But don't commit the mistake Anita did. Speak up for yourself. If she would've spoken about it earlier, those evildoers would have got punishments and lessons that they deserved.

No one has the right to exploit you.

No one has the right to kill your dreams.

You can dream and achieve anything. If you believe in yourself, anything is possible!

STORY TEN

MY DARKEST THOUGHTS

by Colby Hobson

I am going to present to you an entry in a journal I found. It appears that a young man was experiencing some glitches in his reality. Let's see how it plays out.

A book opens and he begins reading.

Hi, my name is Dillan and I've been having some weird thoughts lately. You see, well I don't know how to say this lightly, but I killed my parents. At least I think I did. Let me start by saying that I'm not sure if I did but there are people saying I did. Okay, let me go back a bit. I was a normal 17-year-old, in a normal school, living a normal life. I didn't have many friends and I'm not very memorable. Other than that, I'm just normal. I live in a house close to Cheshire Park and one day everyone began acting weird. I know most of the people in the area so I know their routines and the way they speak. Until just last week, when I noticed my neighbour, Susan, playing with a dog. You must be wondering what's so weird about it. Well, for one, she is deathly allergic to dogs. Last time she was even around one, she ended up in the hospital for 3 weeks. For her safety, I ran over and asked her why she was playing with a dog. She looked at me confusingly and just stared at me. I called for an ambulance and when they came, they took the dog instead. I kept pushing them, asking why they were taking the dog instead of Susan. Now I love my neighbour and she's always been the nicest to me, but after the ambulance drove off, she said something that got me confused.

"Oh, hi, Dillan. When did you get here?"

I explained to her what happened and she said she didn't remember playing with a dog. She was sitting on her porch just to relax. I told her I must be going crazy and I just walked away. Ever since then, I've felt like I'm being watched. Not just outside but in my own house and even the bathroom. I even have a hidey-hole in the back of my closet that I go into when my parents argue. They both have loud voices and I'm usually a quiet person. Anyway, anywhere I went slowly began turning weird. The trees wouldn't move when there was wind blowing. Not even people's clothes moved when they walked. It was like looking at a character from a video game that isn't fully animated. People would stare at me and it would be dead silent, even during rush hour. After that, I refused to step foot outside. My parents became worried and called, what was it, a psychiatrist? I told him everything about what's been going on and he told me that I may have a case of both paranoia and maybe schizophrenia. I knew it can't be that, I just know it! I even talked to my friend Aiden and his friend Ashley about it.

"I admit, I've been feeling the same way. Like all of sudden, everyone just began acting weird." Aidan said while rubbing the back of his head. Ashley jumps in seeming a bit worried, "When we were driving to the store the other day, I felt watched."

"And you're normally not worried about that. You like being the centre of attention," I said jokingly. Ashley laughed, "I agree!"

I'm not the only one feeling this way, so it's not a coincidence. I've been thinking about everything that could be happening, but I don't have a clue. I've been writing down all sorts of stuff that's been going on and... Here I'll share it with you.

Day 1-Eyes

I've been feeling watched for so long and I don't know why. It's everywhere I go. It's like the walls have eyes. I'm beginning to have nightmares about it now. Walls with eyes, people and creatures with more eyes. I feel like I'm going crazy.

Day 2-Frenzy

Some people at school today began acting weird. They were running around, chanting and hollering, and even began to, what looked like, hurt themselves. My parents never noticed them but my friends did.

And that's only two entries! I have plenty of other weird stuff in here too! Like birds pausing in the air, water freezing in warm temperature, and so much more! I just don't understand why everything is happening. I'm going to see my friends and we can try to figure out something together.

After that, it appears that another entry was written only later that day. The last one was written at 12:26 on a Wednesday. This next one was written at 5:12 that same day. This one has stains on the page.

I can't believe it... Aiden is dead. He was hit by a car before school today. He and Ashley went to the park before and on their way there, they were both hit. Ashley says it was out of nowhere when the guy ran a red light and sped off after he hit them. This has to be connected somehow, I just know it! You know, looking back, nothing weird has happened today. Everything was normal again. Did something kill my friend in order to fix things? This can't be right, because I still feel watched. Maybe it's the shock that made things feel normal. Wait! That's it! Giving things a little shock! Maybe I can make others feel normal alongside me with a big shock!

After this, it's been a few days since his last entry. It's interesting how the mind can make things in just a short time. Of course, things can take a while to actually prepare and make it in working order. However, with the right mind and skills, anything can be completed fairly quickly. Being crafty is an amazing skill to have. You can do so much with it. However, you don't want to hear about that, you want to hear about what Dillan did, don't you? Fine, let's move on. This next one is a long one but the final entry.

Time: 11:26 Tuesday

I've done it! After weeks of testing, remodeling, testing, and more remodeling, I'VE FINALLY DONE IT! I just made the best present for my parents. They'll be in complete shock when they find out I did this for them! They'll be so happy they'll be steaming with joy and dancing in pure enjoyment! I think it's time for a pool party, don't you think? I'm so excited! I have to go get Ashley and show her this.

Time: 12:30 Tuesday

What did I do? I went over to Ashley's and she was so worried about me because we haven't spoken in a long while. She made me so mad asking all these questions! I got so mad that I blacked out and woke up outback with a shovel in my hands. I couldn't find Ashley in the house. Maybe she just left and we were gardening? Yes, that's it! I had to have been helping her with her garden. She has been wanting to plant flowers in her backyard so I had to have been helping. So why did I run home scared? Something feels wrong again but I can't put my finger on it. I feel watched again and like something is listening to me and reading my journal. STAY OUT OF MY JOURNAL AND STAY AWAY FROM ME! When I find whatever you are, I'm going to kill you! I will destroy you when I find you! I'm tired of all of this bullshit! Wait wait wait, what am I saying? I'm going nuts.

That's how it all started but I don't remember ANY OF THAT happening. I don't, but these dates are marked as today. In fact, the time currently is 12:38 on this Tuesday. It's weird. Maybe something weird is going on? I need to speak with Aiden and Ashley. Wait, it's written here that Aiden was killed? I don't understand anything anymore. Maybe I should go ask my neighbour. She's playing with a dog and she's deadly allergic. I don't even know why she's playing with one in the first place?

Writing in a journal can help with many things. Letting out emotion, stress, keeping secrets and deep desirables locked away from prying eyes. Too bad with every entry, a part of you is left behind to relive a part of that life forever. Always wondering what that last entry meant and forever changing that moment making a new path over and over. It's called the parallel universe theory. It doesn't work like how you think. You have to do something and complete it in order for a new path to form. Just like young Dillan here. All locked up in his life pod forging thousands of paths along his journey through life.

STORY ELEVEN

THE LAST MOVE

by Suraj Singh Sisodia

"Ugh- that is messed up," said inspector Mhatre looking at the dead body of a woman who looked familiar but he couldn't remember. Nobody heard him in the rain and thunder except...

"Yeah, I know, right?" said officer Fernandez who walked up right beside the inspector, eating an apple. He was not wearing any raincoat like the inspector nor was he carrying an umbrella. He was drenched in the rain. "And we have to work in the rain," he added.

"No, rain is not the problem," inspector clarified, "It's the murderer, I mean look at her."

The officer looked at the dead woman without any interest and nodded. The inspector looked at him in disbelief. He knew that he would have to do all the work on this case too like all the others he worked on with Fernandez.

"Just- just talk to the coroner," he ordered Fernandez.

"On it, sir." He did a little salute thing and walked away.

Mhatre shook his head. This was not how he expected to spend his weekend. He looked at the cloudy, foggy sky, still pouring tiny but piercing droplets of water, making so much noise that almost made everything go quiet. This was what the month of July felt like in Mumbai.

Mhatre had not been in the city for too long. He was just transferred here a year ago and was getting used to everything, that was different from the place he came from. The traffic, local trains and transport buses, the busy life, and people. He hated that he got work almost every weekend. Somebody somewhere got killed or went missing every week. It was like the city was breeding the criminals. He had decided to spend this rainy day in the comfort of his bed or maybe watching a movie but his plans were foiled again when he received a call that a dead body of a woman was found.

When Mhatre got back at the police station, Fernandez was already there.

"Got anything on the dead woman?" asked Mhatre.

"Yeah, the coroner puts the time of death around midnight."

"And the cause of death?"

"Uh..." the officer hesitated, "Loss of blood."

"What?"

The inspector couldn't understand. He pictured the dead woman in his head. She looked like she was beaten up pretty badly, he couldn't understand that she bled to death from those tiny puncture wounds on her neck.

"Yes," replied the officer.

“Are you kidding?”

“That’s what the coroner said.”

“What about the beating?”

“She survived that. Somehow.”

“She bled to death?” Mhatre asked. He still couldn't believe it.

“Yes. The autopsy report will be here by tomorrow morning.”

“How is this even possible? There was not a single drop of blood on the scene. You said the time of death was around midnight, that gives us what- about ten-eleven hours before the rain started. By then the blood would have dried and no rain could have washed that away.”

“I don’t know. Maybe it was a vampire,” replied Fernandez. Mhatre lost his temper.

“IS THIS A JOKE TO YOU?”

“No, I'm sorry.”

Mhatre took a few deep breaths and asked, “Do we have any ID on the victim?”

“Yeah, she didn’t have any wallet on her so we ran her prints just in case and...,” he stopped for a dramatic effect while Mhatre rolled his eyes. “She is Rani, a small-time thief. She was brought in just a week ago.”

And then Mhatre remembered why she looked familiar and suddenly he remembered something else.

“Wasn’t there an accomplice?” he asked.

“Yup. Javed. Got their file right here,” he waved the file before the inspector's face, smiling. This time Mhatre didn’t say anything.

“What’s his last known address?” He asked.

“What? Why?” Fernandez wasn’t smiling anymore.

Mhatre didn’t care to answer his stupid question. He snatched the file out of his hand and looked up the address. He then handed him the file back and started to walk out when Fernandez followed.

“Are you going to arrest him?”

“Maybe. He might have something to do with this.”

“I’ll come with you.”

“That’s okay.”

“Come on, you might need my help. An extra hand is always better.”

Mhatre was in a hurry and didn’t want to argue so he said nothing and they both got in his car and drove away.

Javed lived on the thirteenth floor of a very old building. It was still raining when they reached there.

“Oh it will crumble to dust if I even blow at it,” gurgled Fernandez as he jumped out of the car and looked at the building.

They both reached the thirteenth floor by elevator and walked up to his door. Mhatre rang the doorbell and they waited until a very skinny man who looked half asleep opened the door.

“Yes?” he demanded.

“I am-”

Mhatre couldn’t even finish because the skinny man pushed him so hard that Mhatre wondered how a man that skinny got so much strength. Fernandez ran after him. Mhatre picked himself up. He heard them heading towards the stairs and he ran for the elevator. He was trying to cut him off in the lobby but somehow the elevator stopped at every single floor though nobody was there to step in. When he finally reached the ground floor, disappointed and frustrated, Javed was long gone. He found Fernandez who simply stood there.

"Why would he run?" Mhatre asked.

"He probably recognized you from earlier when you brought them in."

"I wasn't the one who brought them in."

This didn't surprise Fernandez.

"Then maybe it was our faces. I mean it doesn't matter how we dress, our faces scream that we are the police." He chuckled. Mhatre didn't know what to say but he knew what to think.

The next morning when Fernandez reached the police station, Mhatre was already there. It looked like he didn't sleep the whole night. He was reading the autopsy report that lay on the desk in front of him.

"Hey, Fernandez," said Mhatre as soon as he saw him, "Weren't those two involved in a drug deal? It was in their file."

"So?"

"It could be related to that. Maybe something went wrong and they killed her."

"That was like months ago."

"Maybe they just found them now."

"Maybe or maybe not."

Mhatre didn't say anything else. He just sat there, looking at nothing and thinking about something when suddenly the phone on the desk rang. Fernandez reached out and answered. He then simply put the receiver back and let the words out slowly,

"They found Javed's dead body."

Javed was found dead at the exact same spot where Rani was found the previous day. There were the same puncture wounds on his neck and he too had bled to death even though there was not a single drop of blood near his body.

Mhatre couldn't sleep for two nights. He was sitting on his desk on Tuesday morning looking, more like staring at the case files. It was raining even more heavily than the previous day. His head hurt so bad that he couldn't fully open his eyes but he was in deep thoughts. He was planning something.

Suddenly a phone tinkled on his desk. He looked around, it wasn't his text notification sound. He then found Javed's phone in an evidence bag that laid on his desk with the files. He opened the text and read it.

'Meet me at the storage house on 57A, Link Road in an hour.'

Mhatre smiled. He picked up a diary and left the police station.

An hour later, Mhatre stepped into the dark storage room without any windows and whose door wasn't even locked. There was just a light bulb hanging from the ceiling that barely lit up a small area in the centre. He walked in and somebody closed the door behind him which suppressed the noise of the rain. The mysterious figure then pointed a gun at Mhatre who didn't even turn back, but smiled and said, "Fernandez."

Fernandez stepped into the light, still pointing the gun at him, and throwing a cautious look at Mhatre.

"Put your gun down. Now," he ordered the inspector.

"Okay. Okay."

Mhatre pulled out his gun and placed it on the floor. Then he just kept looking at Fernandez and didn't say a word.

"You knew?" Fernandez finally asked.

"I had a hunch."

"How?"

"Oh, I found out about you months ago, my diary is filled with my doubts about you. I knew someone was tipping the gang off before we could make a bust. Patel brought it out at first that how you never got to see a successful drug bust. Only I cared to see this coincidence. We never made a single successful bust after you joined. I knew you had to be the mole. I just didn't have any proof."

Fernandez seemed impressed by Mhatre's work. He didn't say anything because he wanted to listen more.

"But I found out your connection to this case only after I looked in the file. Rani and Javed were involved in that drug deal and then I realized Javed didn't run because he recognized me, he ran because he recognized you."

Fernandez smiled and nodded.

"I just mentioned the drug deal to your face to make you concerned so you make a mistake impulsively trying to kill me too."

"Oh? And what mistake did I make?" Fernandez asked tauntingly.

"This," Mhatre replied as he pulled a second gun, aimed at Fernandez's heart and took a shot.

Fernandez didn't see it coming. He fell back on the floor and stopped moving immediately.

Now it was time for Mhatre to taunt.

"You see, you should always check your enemy for a hidden weapon." He said to the dead officer lying in front of him.

"Oh- okay, will take care of that next time."

Mhatre stopped dead in his spot. He looked at the dead body of Fernandez in horror who rose up slowly and looked straight at him, smiling.

"Ho- how- is this- possible?"

Mhatre couldn't even speak. He stumbled back to the wall. The gun slipped out of his hand out of fear and fell on the floor. He was sweating and breathing heavily. Fernandez just kept smiling.

"Those weren't drugs, those were vials of human blood." He finally said. "There's a lot you don't know about this city. Let me tell you the stories of the underworld."

Fernandez threw the gun away and crouched in front of Mhatre who was curled up on the floor with his back to the wall.

"The underworld is not run by just criminals, it is also run by different families of other creatures of the dark too. Javed and Rani were blackmailing one of the families. We entertained them for a few months but then they started to demand even more. They threatened to expose us. You see Mhatre, there's one thing we want. Privacy. We don't want to kill humans but when it comes to our privacy when someone threatens to expose our secret, we can't tolerate that. We had to kill them."

Mhatre was still fear-stricken but he was listening intently. Fernandez looked at him with pity and said, "I didn't want to kill you, but when you linked the case to that deal, our secret was in danger. I couldn't let that happen. I'm sorry Mhatre but I have to kill you but hey," his eyes lit up and he taunted Mhatre, "You wanted to know how they both died, right? Well, now you'll get to experience it yourself. Any last words?"

Mhatre struggled.

"But- I- I shot you."

"I know. It sucks. You brought a handgun mate. Had you brought a machete or a shotgun and blown my head right off then it would have done something but a bullet, it didn't even tickle. Enough talk. Goodbye Mhatre, I'll miss you."

And then he let out a wild growl and Mhatre saw a whole set of sharp teeth draw out on top of Fernandez's regular ones and felt them plunge into his neck. He saw the light before his eyes fade away as Fernandez sucked his whole blood from his body but when he was an inch away from the death, Mhatre put his last bit of remaining strength to bring a smile on his lips, a faint but certain, a weak but lasting smile.

Fernandez was puzzled to see that smile. He wondered if there was anything he might have missed because he didn't trust Mhatre's clever guts at all and then he remembered.

That night he sneaked in his house and found the diary in the drawer of his nightstand. He was about to burn that down but curiosity got the best of him. He opened it, shuffled a few pages looking for his name or anything at all but it was empty. And then he heard the sound of pumping a shotgun behind him. He smiled.

"Mhatre?" He asked without turning.

"No, his friend," said the man who was pointing the shotgun straight at his face.

Fernandez turned and looked at him.

"Just- just how?" He asked.

"He called me before going to that storage house. He was wearing a wire. He thought he would take all the information about the gang out of you and he knew he might not come back alive."

The man's eyes were sparkling with rage.

"I would've killed you right there but I didn't know how. Mhatre knew that. He tricked you into revealing your weakness."

Fernandez clenched his jaw. His smile had vanished.

"Bastard!" he said under his breath.

"Yeah, it sucks, right?"

"But how'd you find me?"

"Oh that was Mhatre too, he said if something happens to him, and somehow you manage to escape from even me, you'd come here to get this diary. This was his last move."

Fernandez lost his cool now completely, he impulsively jumped on the man but his head was blown off by the shotgun whose sound echoed through the rain and faded away into the night.

STORY TWELVE

ABDUCTED

by Rashi Aggarwal

I am standing on the platform in an utter state of confusion and fear. I can sense the dysphoria rushing through my body. I am just a few moments away from having a panic attack. Since my mother's death, I have been struggling with anxiety and panic attacks, but I don't want to seek any sort of help. I take a few deep breaths and try to hold myself together. I need to do whatever they tell me to do, that's the only way I could save myself from having the same fate as her. I don't know how I landed in this situation and why am I told to travel with this suitcase, why am I even doing this? I have no clue what this suitcase contains. It doesn't feel heavy or anything but I can feel some object moving left to right as I walk. I remember last night being the most horrific night I ever witnessed in my life, felt as if I entered the dark side of journalism way too soon.

A sudden shriek produced by the friction between the train's wheels and the track as the train hits the brakes, hits my ear. The loud horn makes me spiral back to reality. I board the train, walk to the end of the compartment, and sit on the seat beside the window. Unlike the train, my mind isn't still.

I was her intern. She never gave me real work; I didn't exactly even know what story she was working on. All I did was run stupid errands for her. She was my sister's friend and gave me an opportunity to work with her, only because she owed her some sort of favour, I believe. She appeared to be a harsh person and an ignorant boss who didn't care about her own intern. She kind of intimidated me and I somewhat feared her; but she didn't deserve to die. She quite had a reputation of working on stories every journalist stayed away from; scandalous stories about big personalities.

The train starts to move and slowly and slowly increases its speed. Soon the station is left behind and it runs through the suburbs.

I found her in her office. I went to give her coffee. I didn't see her face. Her body was on the floor, facing it, surrounded by blood. I hated fetching her coffee and wished she would just die but I didn't mean it literally. The coffee fell from my hand, spilling all over the floor, splashing on my shoes. I could feel cold sweat running down my face, my underarms drenched with the sweat too. Suddenly, the security rushed in and I was pulled out of the room. It felt as if someone grabbed my arm and dragged me out forcefully. I woke up in a dark alley.

I close my eyes and rest my head against the window. I didn't notice the woman next to me till she started talking randomly. My head is just spinning around and this lady won't stop rambling. I don't want to know about her life or her kids. My head is too occupied contemplating last night's events and trying to figure out all the blurry memories I have. I give her a strange look and go back to staring outside the window. There is a kid with his mom on the platform, she is tickling him and his laughter takes me back to the time my mother made me laugh by tickling my stomach.

I was so lost in my own world that I didn't notice that the woman who is sitting in the seat next to me just zip-tied my hand to the arm of the seat that divided our sitting spaces. I can feel a rush flowing from my feet up to my head and before I could panic, she injected me with something; it felt cold flowing into my veins. I can't feel my arm anymore and later the sensation travels through my body. Everything feels numb. I can't feel my hands, legs or anything. I'm not even able to move a finger.

"Don't worry, this serum has just temporarily paralyzed you, I'm saving you from the bad guys."

My heartbeats increase exponentially while I experience something like a vertigo which leads to ringing in my ear making me feel as if I am going deaf. I don't understand anything. Is this woman behind all this? I have never seen her before in my life. Was my boss working on a story involving her?

I try to move my arms, legs, anything; but nothing works except my eyeballs. I'm sitting on the window seat, that too in the end of the compartment. Even if I try to use my eyes to seek help, I can't. All this adrenaline rush is making me feel dizzy. As the train stops at the next station, the lady grabs the wheelchair she kept against the partition. She places me in it and plays the role of a mother caring for a sick son. I was the first one to board the train so nobody questioned her or gave strange looks. I couldn't even move my face to try to ask for help. Internally, I am screaming and feeling so helpless. We exit the station and move towards the parking. We reach a strange vehicle. The door opens and two men come out of it. There is another man sitting in the driver's seat. They grab the wheelchair and place me in the car. They sit on my either side and all of the sudden cover my face with a black cloth. I feel so suffocated. I haven't talked to my sister since the last night. She must have texted me. She must have called for help feeling I'm in danger. She knows I'll never ignore her call. People must be looking for me and I know I'll be ok. Hope was the only thing that could keep me sane.

As the cloth creates an abyss around me, flashbacks play in my mind. It feels like someone is manipulating my mind and making me watch random clips of my mother and me. I feel as if I know them all but these memories are vague. I do remember that she used to sing lullabies to me every night. Her voice was so angelic. She loved to dress me every morning. Every time she took me out of shower, I used to wear my towel like a cape and wait on my bed till she picked out my outfits. I miss the way she gently combed my hair and then parted them to the left side calling me her sweet baby boy. She was the most beautiful, gentle and kindest woman in my life. I was 5 when she died, they say it was tuberculosis. Dad took the responsibility after mum; but one day, out of nowhere, he just vanished. He came home drunk and this behavior soon became a routine. My sister became the adult of the house. She dropped out of school to start working so she could put me through school and college. Though, I decided to work after graduating from high school. I decided to take the journalism internship, later on, to make sure it was what I wanted.

I am just linking my mother's death and Sonia's death, which is a murder, together. Am I the reason for their deaths? My mother's TB doesn't explain her death at all and Sonia died when I started working for her. And, I'm here, kidnapped...I can be wrong but I'm the one who's kidnapped. I'm sure there must be some link.

“Don't worry, if you die, you'll be of no use and I will be killed too. You are safe with us.” Her sudden words breaking the silence, startles me giving me a little jump.

"The reporter was working on a story about Godmother's men. They killed your boss and those nincompoops chose you to do their dirty work. You are special, my boy. Godmother killed those idiots and asked me to fetch you."

I couldn't believe what I just heard. But at the same time, nothing surprises me anymore. I have no clue how I can be of such value to Godmother. She is the most wanted criminal. She has been involved in numerous murders and countless people going missing but nothing concrete has ever been found against her.

I can feel the effect of the serum wearing off. I am able to move my fingers and slowly gain sensation in my arms and legs. My limbs seem to have fallen asleep and it hurts to move, even my toes.

The vehicle stops and the two men push me out of the vehicle. I drop to my knees with my hands on the ground seeking support. I'm still not completely out of the serum's effect. I struggle to get up and the men forcefully grab one arm each.

"Tell your freaking monster to leave me alone. I don't want to be her boy toy." I said as I shrugged and forcefully freed my hands from the men.

"Shut your mouth or you'll get us all killed," the lady spoke as she removed my mask. The bright light enters my eyes which is not really comfortable.

I stand still and observe the building. It is grey and looks like a huge cuboid. The exterior seems to be made of steel and coated with paint. It is a warehouse, a warehouse, in the middle of nowhere.

As we walk through the warehouse, I notice a lot of strange-looking men with huge guns in their hands staring us up and down. These men look dead from outside; as if they are some sturdy robots. We all are just walking straight ahead. This walk feels never-ending.

Suddenly, out of nowhere, some men appear in front of us and encircle us. It just startled me and the lady gave a small shriek. I guess she wasn't expecting this either and starts to blabber.

"No, No! I'm done with my job. Don't do this. Why are you even doing this? I haven't done anything. I got the boy. Take the boy. Leave me!"

I stare at her and my anxiety shoots up. She got us all in a hostage situation, that too under the most dangerous person in the world. The men dragged and pushed us into something that looked like a cage for big animals. They locked us inside it. The lady slams her body against the rods of the cage screaming and falls back. Right now, my mind is numb and I don't even care about what happens next anymore. The bad thoughts unravel in my mind.

I come out of my zone as I hear the footsteps approaching. I know who it is. With each footstep, my heartbeat escalated. A cold sweat ran all over my face. Before I even looked up, the lady slammed against the bars hailing Godmother, begging her to redeem her, forgive her. I have no idea what she did so wrong. I heard a thud as if she was hit really hard on her head and she fell on the floor beside me. I look at her first and then I look up.

As I look up, I'm taken aback and I stare in disbelief. A few words come out of my mouth.

"It's you, you're alive!"

"Hello, son."

STORY THIRTEEN

ENOUGH

by CF Gonzi

"Where are you going?"

"I just want to be alone."

"But where? There's not many places to be alone here."

"That's why I'm leaving."

"Hmm. It's such a beautiful day. You could stay outside?"

"Yeah. I think I probably will for this."

"OMG, did you see that pigeon?"

"You mean the billions of pigeons? They're everywhere. All the time. What's new?"

"That one, just beyond the fence. It has gold in its feathers."

"I'm sorry, did you see that? Or do I need to roll my eyes again?"

"Come on, don't you just want to relax and enjoy the day? You could always put it off."

"I don't think it's possible for me to enjoy things anymore, so I might as well get it over with now."

"What do you mean?"

"Gee, I don't know, maybe the fact that getting out of bed in the morning is the hardest thing in the world? Or that just standing to take a shower is exhausting, not to mention pointless. I mean, have you seen me today?"

"I thought you were killing the grunge look."

"Yeah, right. I don't kill any looks."

"You really think so?"

"It's how I feel. It has nothing to do with what I think."

"I don't know if I agree with you on that one."

"Does it matter if we agree?"

"I guess not. Oh, wow, did you see that convertible?"

"Ugh, so noisy. Why would anyone drive that?"

"Why not? Anyway, where are you headed?"

"Just further into the city."

"Hey, good idea. People watching is so fun in the city."

"You know I'm not going for the people."

"You're right, sorry. So, why the city?"

"Just to get as far away from home and school as possible, I guess."

"Well, if you're trying to be secretive, you should tuck that knife further into your pants."

"Shit. You can see it?"

"Anyone with eyes could see that."

"How about this?"

"Yeah, that should work. But, why are you doing this?"

"I want it to end. That's all."

"Everything?"

"Everything."

"Why?"

"You're kidding. There are too many reasons to count. Didn't you hear mom? She hates me. She thinks it's my fault dad left."

"Did she tell you that?"

"Well, no. But you've seen the way she looks at me."

"Uh-huh. I guess you're right, she definitely doesn't treat you the same."

"Right? She doesn't even want me around the house anymore. And quite frankly, when she starts drinking, I don't want to be there anyway."

"Don't blame you on that one."

"And I know you heard what Marissa said in English."

"Which part? She had quite a bit to say to you once Mr. Bishop left the room."

"The 'you don't deserve to live' part."

"Oh, yeah. I can't believe she said that to you, just because she's jealous."

"She's not jealous. She's right! There's no point to my life, so why live?"

"Hey, STOP! Watch where you're going, that bus almost hit you."

"I don't even care anymore."

"Yes, you do, or you wouldn't have stopped."

"You just startled me. Now, hurry up."

"Anyway, Marissa is a narcissistic hag. You know she was just mad because you hit her in the face with that football in PE and it made Brett laugh. You're really going to take what she said seriously?"

"It's not just her. It has been going on for years and I know everyone thinks so. I don't even have any real friends anymore. They've all got boyfriends or clubs or better friends than me taking up all their time. I have nothing."

"What are you talking about? Phoebe just invited you to her party on Saturday. Unless, ah! You think she was just pitying you?"

"Of course that's what it was. She literally told me she noticed I was alone more often than before when she gave me the effing invite."

"I can't really argue with that. But hey, you do have me."

"You don't count."

"Ouch. Hey, why'd you stop?"

"I don't know. This looks like a good spot, I guess."

"Wait, hold on a minute. You're not even going to try to get through this?"

"There's no point to trying. It doesn't get better."

"But you haven't tried going to a therapist."

"Therapy is witchcraft—Dad said so himself."

"They could prescribe you medication."

"I'm not going to depend on drugs if they don't even work."

"You don't know that, you haven't even tried them."

"I'm not going to. Not when it would be so much easier to just end it."

"You think this is easier?"

"It is for me."

"No good trying to change your mind then."

"Nope."

"But can you at least do it somewhere pretty? Not in this awful alleyway?"

"Does it really matter?"

"That's up to you. Do you want the last thing you see to be this brick wall?"

"I guess not. Where would you suggest, then?"

"Let's go up to the meadow. There're tons of wildflowers this time of year—it's beautiful. A fitting place to die."

"Yeah. . .yes, I think I'd like that."

"Plus, it's only about a block away from here. You won't have to suffer much longer."

"Even better. Let's go."

"Sweet, follow me. Aw, look at that cute couple!"

"Gross. I am so sick of couples."

"I think you're just sick of being alone."

"I actually rather enjoy being invisible. Now, keep walking and avoid eye contact."

"I guess the beauty of being invisible is that they will just ignore you, too."

"Exactly."

"Hm. It's such a beautiful day."

"Would you quit saying that?"

"At least it will be warm. Wasn't your worst fear freezing to death?"

"Ha, yeah, I guess it was at one point. Hey, isn't the meadow—"

"This is the shortcut Dad showed us years ago, remember?"

"Huh. No, I don't remember. When did he show us this?"

"You know, that day we were going to pick flowers for mom? He said if we turned right after we saw the church's steeple, we would get there faster than taking the sidewalk."

"I seriously have no memory of this."

"Don't you want to just get it over with already?"

"Yes."

"Then come on. Trust me."

The doors to the emergency room couldn't open quick enough. Setting my knife on the counter, I wrestled with myself to make eye contact through my tears with the shocked nurse.

"I need help."

STORY FOURTEEN

THE CRIPPLED SOUL

by Srishti Sareen

Amara is just like any other girl you would ever meet. She has beautiful light brown eyes just like the honey sparkling under the sun. Her curly black hair is entangled just like her soul. She is eighteen now and it's the last year of her school. She is an introvert and she never connected with any other student in her batch, but still, boys started drooling over her by not even knowing her. She surely is a quiet little statue in her class whose existence was negligible since her childhood. So the little girl grew up alone without any friends or family but no one knew that the innocent face had some darkness developing inside her. Whenever a guy tried to interact with her, she would just walk away leaving behind a sense of curiosity that how one can behave like a mute puppet. Who knew she actually was a puppet whose strings were tackled strictly by a dark parasite living inside her, who consumed her soul and triggered her emotions.

Amara's beauty was indeed everlasting, guys kept staring at her but she never reacted to anyone. Even the girls of her class were jealous of how she could be the centre of attraction even though she did nothing to lure anyone. No one knew that Amara lived alone in an apartment and the reason was hidden from each and every person. She herself was unaware of how that loneliness turned into darkness.

At times Amara felt a crackling chill down her spine making her believe that something living inside her is more powerful than her soul. The thing left her as cold as if she was on her deathbed. The bright purple light inside her brain that was intact through all these years is now more visible to her. Earlier she just had glimpses of that light for some seconds and then it would just vanish out of her sight. The purple light that controlled her and is the door of blackness for her soul, which is now caged inside that blackness. It was weird for her to accept that the light inside her brain was growing stronger every second. The purple light overpowered Amara and forced her to start killing animals to quench its thirst.

Amara was restless and felt it hard to help herself anymore, as if she was just a pawn, who had to satisfy the needs of that purple light inside her. The light led her on the path to kill. First, she killed a lizard and this series of killing innocent animals continued. She even killed her own cat Coffee. She never enjoyed killing animals and tried to stop that push of the purple light. Every time she tried that, she scared herself. The bruises were even more prominent in that case so she had to agree to the demon inside her. And this way she ended up opting the bloodbath of innocent animals. She never faced the purple light in front of her. Those glimpses she had, now they were just some blurry visions that lasted for some minutes now and each time she satisfied the urge she was a step closer to the purple light, to know who is the one controlling her. That silent demon was sturdy and convinced her to do whatever it wanted.

But recently Amara started hearing some whispers about what to do and how to do things. It was all happening as if she was hypnotized by the purple light itself. This dark secret was concealed because the demon sealed her tongue every time she tried to spill the beans or craved to pour the whole load off her shoulders. Her tongue was sealed as if someone grabbed it so that she can't say anything, even her back had scratches. Earlier she always buried the dead animal, but now she is harsh and the demon got hold of her hands; it just brutally crushed the body. The demon started whispering what Amara should do:

"I know who you are and I have experienced your instincts, continue it till you fulfil my thirst, otherwise I'll have to scratch you and will leash you in this cage."

Amara was terrified because she couldn't ignore the demon's urge to lead her to the mirror and to show who it really was inside her head. All of this happened when Amara was eight years old, the glowing purple light appeared suddenly at the night of her birthday and hypnotized her to follow the rules in order to see the mirror and find out about the person with the sparkling purple light, inside her brain. The curious little kid started doing the things the demon asked for and did everything secretly. It's been ten years now and till now no one knows about the sinful deeds done by Amara. She felt bad but still was relieved that there was silence in her head for some time until she was given another task, to find its prey and kill it. Every time she killed a living creature, she was full of guilt and remorse. The moment she started crying the demon would say:

"These living creatures have lived their lives, you should just kill them mercilessly. Do not ever regret what you did, just think that you gave it a purpose to be born again as a new species."

The thought clicked Amara that the demon was right and she should not be guilt-ridden and persuade herself to do as the purple light directs her to. Now killing the animals, snapping their necks, poking them with knives, tearing them apart was nothing for her. She did it whenever she wanted to and was now ruthless. It all happened like the pawn is now the Queen, who can kill anyone off the board. The old soul was buried alive somewhere deep inside, the one which had some sense of what it feels like to be damaged this way. She started going out every night and found animals so that she could kill and burn them. She would wear black clothes and cover her face with a mask. She carried a bag with her, filled with knives, gasoline in little cans and lighters. The darkness was driving her to the top of a cliff and left her there to hang on that edge. Not even a single day passed by when she missed murdering an animal. She missed the demon that overpowered her, it is the weirdest thing one can miss. But the only thing in her life was that bright purple light around her. The more she killed the more she wanted to face the demon. She wanted to know who actually was forcing her to pursue this road of madness. When she burned the three kittens, the demon appeared and said:

"I think you are really enjoying killing these animals and you want to see the mirror now and know who has the strings of a little puppet like you."

She never tried to interact with the demon but it understood what her silence meant. Now that Amara was in front of the mirror, she was there for hours altogether. Not even a single glimpse came in front of her, the moment she was about to leave with her bag pack, the demon said:

"You gave up so soon young lady, the memories need time to get framed and portrayed in that mirror. You lived with me in this darkness for ten years and now you are leaving the mirror. Go back to the room and stand in front of the mirror. You will see why and how this all started."

The moment she stepped back the purple light murmur,

That she has nothing else in her life to nurture.

She is now going to be aware that who is behind the plan,

The plan that forced her to kill the whole clan.

She will see who was the possessor of the darkness that prevailed inside her somewhere deep,

The one who just left her; without her once existing peaceful sleep.

That tumbled her soul over a year,

And left her just like a carcass thrown aside under a sheet.

She was standing there and in one's own good time a blurry image of a woman and man appeared who were fighting over something and a little kid was hidden under a table. In no time the whole image was visible, the mirror displayed her own mother and father fighting over a misunderstanding and Amara was hiding under the table. Her father was accusing her mom of having an extramarital affair with her brother-in-law. It was her eighth birthday and under that table, she saw them fighting again. He always used to abuse her and she already had bruises over her body. Her father was short-tempered and Amara had seen him beating her up, pouring hot boiling water over her. She was always scared of her father. That night her father killed her mother and he made Amara see her mom's body burning up. The whole scene was in front of her eyes once again after ten years, her eyes were filled with tears and she couldn't stop crying. She couldn't save her mother then and can't save her now. She was terrified of seeing the portion of what she was forced to experience back then. Her father was a drunkard and asked Amara to put a knife through his heart and push him in the hole he dug for himself and bury him. He left a letter to her daughter and asked her to give it to her uncle. Her birthday was ruined, she saw her mother turning into ashes then murdered her own father and buried him. The letter never said anything specific about what happened that night. It only mentioned his brother to live with Amara and take care of her. Her uncle lived with her and only left her when she turned ten. He took care of her expenses but never met her in person.

The darkness started growing inside as a child, the murderous character developed because of her own family's stupidity that killed the once existing innocence in her. That innocence was caged inside the bright purple light inside her brain that consumed her soul.

STORY FIFTEEN

WE WERE ON THE SAME PAGE

by Ayush Aggarwal

I landed in this city a month ago. I was in awe of it as soon as I got off the plane. The midnight blue of the sky in the evening, the brusque cool wind trying to carry me away with its flow, the youth of the city calling out to me and the constant drizzling was enough for me to fancy it. I don't know why I am writing this letter or whether somebody would ever get a hold of it or not. In the last one month of my life, I had only managed to scrape out one friend out of this city and that is Vritti. She's almost a local as she lives on the outskirts of this city. Both of us come from moderately rich and extensively conservative families, maybe that was the reason that we actually became friends. I had been a socially awkward person all my life, minding my own business, sitting in classes with my head down in the books and studying as if that would make me get over the fact that I practically had no friends in my school. But I had a dog that I loved more than anything in this world, my precious Bruno; overdosing on love and food, furry and bulky beagle dog. Bruno was the only thing that made my life back home tolerable. I came from a small town of Ludhiana to this euphoric city of Pune in search of adventures and fun that I had been deprived of all my life because of the overprotective nature of my family and my own social anxiety. Vritti and I have had a lot of fun in the past couple of weeks, we went shopping for dresses, she made me try out the elegant cafes of this city, we pretty much spent all of our days together. My hostel curfew was at 10 PM, so we used to hang out in the city till that and then she took a cab home and I used to sit in my room and take pride over the fact that at last, I too have made a friend. But I still had a dream unfulfilled, I still had something inside of me aching. I had always fantasized about the exemplary nightlife of this town. And now that I was here, I wanted to experience it. Vritti was a bit skeptical of it, "What will we tell our parents?" She used to ask and I really had no answer for that. Because I too had to get my mom to call the warden of the hostel in order to get a night off. And then one Friday evening I came up with a devious little plan. By this point, I had told my mom all about Vritti, how she was a local, how she had become my best friend and how her mom was the sweetest person and packed up lunch for both me and her with native Marathi food during the college days. Basically, I made my Punjabi mom fall in love with her. So I just told my mom that it was her birthday the next day and I was going to spend the next night over at Vritti's home, and I suggested Vritti do the same. She told her mom that it was my birthday and she was going to spend the next night over with me at my hostel. Both of our mothers, innocent and trusting their little girl's words gave us the permissions for a sleepover, for the first time in both of our lives.

It was 6pm, and the dusk was just setting in and both of us met just outside my hostel with bags at our back and the city at our feet. We had booked ourselves a hotel room to crash at later, and also to get ready before going out and winning the night over. We donned our hottest dresses, put on some makeup, wore our heels and walked out of the hotel at 9:30pm sharp, to bring our dreams into reality. We went to this club called "Scandal" in the Koregaon Park area. It held the wildest party every weekend in Pune; also, it was the most expensive club in the city. But money was never an issue for both of us thanks to the love of our parents. The one thing that we did not know was that "Scandal" did not allow stag entries, even for girls. You had to have a date to get into this place, but sadly we did not have any. We tried our best to bribe our way in, but in vain. And just as all hopes were lost there came these two handsome gentlemen; and by gentlemen, I mean actual men. They looked nothing short of 30, both looked like they were in the corporate sector, well-combed hair, with their casual suits on and utter fair complexion came in as angels and saved the night. One of them went, "Hi ladies, I'm Prateik and this is Vaibhav. We need a date to get into this party, and we cannot find anybody better than you around here. So, would you like to go in with us?" I, being a stupid kid, just started blushing cluelessly; because this wasn't only the first time I was asked out. This was the first time somebody showed any kind of interest in me and that too not for study notes. And also both of these guys were incredibly hot and somehow, Prateik had this confident vibe going on around him, almost as if he knew that he had me at "hi ladies." It was like at that moment I discovered vistas of infatuations and attraction within myself that I didn't even know existed before. Vritti mustered up all the courage she had and with a broad smile said "Yeah, sure." As soon as we stepped in, the pungent smell of alcohol took me by surprise. I had never been inside a nightclub before. And it was every bit of insane and dreamy as I thought of it to be. There were people doing shots, slobbering all over each other, girls grinding their partners, guys trying to hit on random girls. It was as if I was transpired into another realm of drunken stupors and dancing fiestas. We headed straight to the bar, now let me clear one thing up; I've only ever drunk twice in my life before that night, and that too with my dad just for the sake of my curiosity. And Vritti, well, she had never really touched alcohol ever. But we were ready to go wild that night. Vaibhav took Vritti a few steps ahead at the bar counter and I was with Prateik at the other side of the bar counter; he bought me a beer. I did insist on paying for my own drink, but he refused with chivalry. I drank the beer one sip at a time at first. I was drinking beer for the first time. I remember, "I like me better" by Lauv was being played by the DJ. I don't know whether it was the music or company of such an interesting guy that after a while, I started gulping the beer down. We started talking, me and Prateik. He told me that he and Vaibhav worked for some bank in the city. I could have listened to him go on about his life all night long; it wasn't that his stories were very intriguing but every time he talked. He had to come closer to my ear and as his ecstatic breath brushed past my neck, a chilling sensation ran down my spine. Every time he leaned in, my heart skipped a beat, every cell inside my body called out for more, it was with great difficulties that I had composed myself in such close proximity with him. Slowly a beer turned into two, then he called for vodka shots and then I gulped down some whiskey, neat. And then I kind of lost the track of time with this amazing person. I found myself in the arms of Prateik, slow dancing on Shawn Mendes' "Never Be Alone." He asked me if I wanted to smoke, at that point of time, I would've said yes to pretty much anything. So, we went on the roof to have a smoke. It was raining so we stood under the shed curled up against each other. He lit up a cigarette in the most fascinating way anyone could. I don't know everything he did was alluring, the way he held my hand through the crowd of teenagers, the way his hands touched my waist while we were dancing, the way he talked, there was something so civil about his manners that I couldn't help but feel drawn towards this gentle soul. He made me take my first ever puff of a cigarette and I literally felt the whole world revolve around my head for a second there. I fumbled and he held my waist and pulled me closer to him. It felt so safe, so warm, so right. I started leaning in towards his face. He was a gentleman. He pulled himself away and said, "I will not take advantage of you, you're drunk right now. I don't want you to regret this when you wake up tomorrow." I was embarrassed and yet falling in love with him at the same time. He told me that we should get out of there and that he was going to drop me off to my hotel as I was too drunk to call a cab for myself. He told me that he'd call me up in the afternoon and we'll go have lunch or something, or that is what I remember. I was really hammered. That's the last thing that I remember from that night. I totally forgot about Vritti and pushed off with him, alone.

Today, the rain is relentless. I hear it thrumming on the metal roof and running down the broken pipe into the mud, and I moisten my cracked lips with my tongue. I wonder if they'll bring me food and water. I wonder if they're coming at all. I wonder who they are. I wonder how I ended up at this abandoned place. I don't even know what day it is, because it's dark outside, and it's raining hard and it almost feels like it's been ages since I've had a drop of water. I don't know if I should shout for help, or just keep quiet and wait for somebody to come by and tell me what is going on. I am locked up from outside so somebody must've put me here for a reason. I don't know anything, I don't have my purse or my phone, I am shabbily dressed. I don't even know where my friend Vritti is. I have not seen her ever since I went upstairs to smoke a cigarette. I don't even know the magnitude of the problem I am in right now. I just know I miss home so bad right now, maybe mom was right, home is safe, she was right all along. I think of Bruno in this time of distress; I think what he might be doing, he must be sleeping, what else does he ever do? The state is so horrible that I can't even cry, I know I should cry, I should scream for help, I should do something rather than writing this all in a torn-up register that I found lying around here with a ball pen. But the thing is it feels like it's all my fault. It feels like I deserve this for lying to my loving parents. It feels like I've spoilt not just one but two lives, Vritti's and mine. I should've just stayed at the hostel and enjoyed all that I had. I should've never tried to be somebody I'm not, I should've never tried to find happiness in strange places with strange people. What will mom think? How disappointed will she be in me, when she realizes I lied to her and went out and did something that I was clearly not supposed to do. I don't know, it hurts, my head hurts, my stomach aches. My whole body is slowly disintegrating, I feel immense magnitudes of perturbed pain inside of me. I feel something eating me up from the inside out. I am feeling pain in places that I cannot describe. It almost feels like something horribly wrong has happened to me, I cannot even fathom to describe the pain I am in. I think I don't want to be found, I want to stay lost. For I cannot bear this pain any longer.

~ Myra. :)

It's been two years, since I found the dead body of this innocent girl along with my team in an abandoned warehouse in a town named Talegaon just outside Pune. And this letter was found lying next to her, and that image still haunts me at night. Both of these girls, Vritti and Myra were raped and left to die at different locations. Fortunately, we got to Vritti before she was consumed by death. But this girl Myra, we could've saved her too. But she cut her wrist off with a broken glass bottle before we could get to her.

She thought that it was her fault that a couple of inhumane pedophiliac vultures chose her as their victim that night. It's horrifying how our society dented a child's psychology so much so that even though she was a victim, she felt as a culprit. Her mind had possibly endured all the extant torment and agony in those lonely hours, and in the end, she just decided to just give it all up. Not because she didn't think that she could be saved, but because she did not want to be saved. Never have I ever let my professional life affect my personal life, being in police. We come across the strangest and sickest of people on a daily basis. But the letter by this lonely little girl shook the deepest manifolds inside my heart. She was so guilty ridden about lying to her parents that instead of facing them, she decided to walk into the realm of the dead. This letter of hers was found by me, and I did not record it in official evidence, as I was supposed to. Mainly because I did not want to be the one to tell her parents that they scared their only daughter off, so much so that she killed herself before the help arrived. And also, because I wanted to charge those delirious pedophiles (Sharad and Peter) - those were their real names – with the most severe sentence. A bit unprofessional? I know. But I am the father of a teenage daughter and I cannot really stand by and watch some pricks take apart the life of someone else's daughter. And in this country, sadly; rape is not crime enough to get a life sentence, you have to be charged with murder for that. And that was exactly what I did, but it did not bring me peace, it didn't bring peace to Vritti, her family and of course, Myra's family. In a way, that day Vritti lost her life too, she lost her innocence to this cruel world, this cruelty which often puts up a civilized facade but is rotten to the very core. I think, nobody was at fault in this whole case but those two imprudent, sick-minded criminals. Myra's parents wanted to save her from the reality of this wretched world of ours, Myra wanted to explore the beauty of the night as glorified by the great poets and writers over centuries and Vritti, well, she just wanted to have some fun with her only friend in college.

STORY SIXTEEN

SILENT STAB

by Kriti Mediratta

Sitting on the sofa, I was staring at the coffee cup kept on the table wondering how far I have come and how drastically things have changed. At that point, the sound of the key unlocking the door bought me back to reality. The door opened and Sara shouted, "We are back from school" and there stood these four beautiful children - Sara, Niya, Fiyaz and Naksh. If you are thinking that they are my children then I would like to tell that biologically they aren't but otherwise they are my whole world. Staying with them for the past two years has really changed my life, neither they had anyone in this selfish world and nor did I. It was a series of unfortunate events in my life which ended with me coming and staying here in this orphanage as a Mother to these homeless but amazing children. They have the purest souls with no secrets and are full of innocence. What world makes of them in the future, that I cannot predict but for now I want to guide them to walk the right path.

I can understand their pain because I lost my parents at the age of 13 in a car accident and that was one of the days when my world came crashing down in front of my eyes. Many say I didn't lose anything because I had a massive empire to inherit but people usually realize it later that money just brings temporary happiness but that's what the world has taught us at every step of our lives -that money is the ultimate priority and this greed makes people do crazy things.

At age of 21, I took over the family business and the people who helped me from the time I lost my parents were the house help family who used to live with us even before I was born and my parent's friends - The Nigams. The house help family included a couple, Bindi and Govind and their son Savir who was a few years younger to me. The Nigams were a very loving family to be around. Tanav uncle took care of my finances and all other little things, he even offered me to stay with them after my parents died but I chose to go to a boarding school. He has two twin daughters Suchi and Simra and I was friends with both of them as they are of my age and I was very fond of them but after I shifted to boarding school, I lost touch with them. Varsha aunty always welcomed me with love as she was best friends with my mother. This was the family I depended on during my loss.

After I joined the business my whole focus was to learn and grow the business to keep the family name alive. Abhay was the Vice President of the business under my father and he handled everything exquisitely till the time I completed my studies, after which he trained me and believed in me to run the business well. At first, it was difficult to make my space there because everyone was treating me like someone who didn't earn the place and position at the office and during those times Abhay supported me and stood for me and with time I was able to prove myself. It was an architecture business and within a year of my joining we were making more profit than ever and bringing many contracts. The employees were also happy and I was happy more than ever, but that happiness was short-lived because soon it started to all go lower. We weren't getting any new contracts and our existing clients started to leave us. We also found out that our company's designs were being leaked to the competitors. In those difficult times, Suchi came to work for me and said, "We will secure our work more and everything will just be fine." She gave me just the support I needed because sometimes all you need is someone to stand beside you in your difficult times.

It had been three days since I had any sleep. A very important bid was in the way and the presentation and design needed to be the best so Suchi and I were working every minute of the day to make this deal happen. We were done with most of the work and it was four in the morning, I told Suchi that it's time we take a break and meet up in the evening for a final check since the presentation was the next day itself. I collected all my documents and headed home. Bindi was awake and she gave me some food to eat after which I went to my room thinking about how badly I needed a nap.

I woke up with a very weird sound and felt a strange smell hit my nose. I realized something was different. I opened my eyes and saw that I was in a hospital. Suchi came to me and told me that I have been asleep for two days - low sugar and low blood pressure was the reason. I asked her about the contract and she told me that she tried but the other company won it. I remembered drinking my coffee with lots of extra sugar, but I assumed that the lack of sleep and careless eating habits got me here.

After coming back home I took a week off to rest. Abhay used to come to the house every day to check up on my health and to update me on how well Suchi was taking care of everything at the office and I thought how lucky I was to have such supportive friends who are also colleagues. It had been around four months since my hospital incident and things were going smoothly, though the business was slow. I had a feeling of satisfaction and happiness. I was working alongside Abhay and Suchi who cheered me up all the time while working. I had started to stay more nights at the Nigam house and Simra was such a joy and was always entertaining everyone by practicing her acting skills and played scenes from her theatre plays and Varsha aunty, she cooked amazing dishes for me. Staying there with them as a part of the family was filling up the feeling of emptiness and loneliness in me.

One day I was staying up late in the office to complete some work when my laptop started giving me security alerts and breach warnings. Luckily, the IT expert Manan was still in the office so I went to him with my laptop. He quickly did some checks and told me that my mail was tampered with and it looked like emails had been sent to an unsecured outside network. Finally after waiting for I don't even know how many minutes or hours, he finally recovered the deleted files from the backup server and gave me the laptop. Reading those emails made me confused and shocked, there were emails sent to the rival company with all our designs and ideas. I saw a mail which brought this gush of a panic attack because that mail was a takeover deal sent by the rival company and then a series of negotiation mails disclosing every small business strategy of my company was there. It was all too much to process so I took my laptop, walked towards the parking area and called Suchi to come to my house immediately and bring Abhay with her. I drove towards my house with my heart beating so fast and my lungs gasping for air as I had just finished climbing 20 floors of stairs. Everything felt like chaos, a big mess whose beginning and the end seemed like a mystery because the emails were sent from my email id.

I felt a tiny relief when I reached my house and a small faith that I would fight my problems with all the strength I had but I had no clue of what was about to hit me next. I unlocked the door to my house and screamed when I saw bodies of Bindi, Gokul and Savir laying still beside the dining table. Blood was gushing out from their throats and mouths, a big puddle of blood was formed around them and then I saw Abhay and Suchi standing next to these innocent bodies wearing gloves and holding knives in their hands. Suchi rushed towards me and banged the door to close behind me and Abhay pointed the knife at me to stop me from escaping or moving. Suchi told me that they don't want to hurt me but I have to sign the takeover papers and give them all my money otherwise they would kill me too or they would blame these murders on me and make me rot in jail for life. At that moment the doorbell rang and I got a tiny hope for a second but Tanav uncle and the IT expert Manan both entered the house with big smiles on their faces. That last hope in me also died.

Everything was clear to me now that I had fallen in the trap set by these greedy murderers. All the things that I used to consider love and support were just the sweet talk to lure me. Now I had to choose between dying, perish in jail or live with a lost fortune. I choose to give up my business, my house and my money as a cost for my life. I signed all the papers giving everything up and then I had to give a false statement to the police about the murders in my house. I told them that I was working in the office and when I reached back the door was unlocked, things scattered and the house help family, they all were dead already. The police filled it as a case of mugging and moved on but I still couldn't move on from what I had faced. It was like my world came crashing down once again and now I had nothing left. I had to decide on what to do next because I had no family, no friends, no money and even no place to stay but what hurt the most was I had no trust to give or courage to fight left in me.

I remembered that some weeks ago I met some people who came to me from an orphanage to ask for a donation and they told me how they were working hard to provide so many orphans with a place to stay, food and even a sense of family in their new town system. I knew that was the place for me to go to now because like those orphans I too had no one in this world because life had made me an orphan once again.

I served my children with a home-cooked hot lunch and their smiles were enough for me to forget my misery and listen to how their day at school was.

STORY SEVENTEEN

SOME QUESTIONS WILL ALWAYS REMAIN UNANSWERED

by Adyasha Mishra

Amelia brewed a pot of coffee on a cold winter morning somewhere in London. Amelia Mathews, a 20-year-old young, beautiful girl who lived in a bungalow near River Thames. She lived in a nuclear family with her dad, mother and elder brother. Oh! Not to forget the 5th member of her family, Coco. She was the most beautiful Siberian Husky dog one would've ever seen.

Amelia was a Designing student. She loved her work. As it was a Sunday, she was free and contemplating by looking outside her window. Suddenly, she decided to clean her old trunk box which consisted of some greeting cards, pictures and a lot of miscellaneous stuff.

She took an old towel to dust out the box. The trunk box looked like an antique piece of some museum. It seemed to have formed a lot of rust all over it. But somehow, Amelia managed to open it and was able to witness a lot of cute stuff inside. Her eyes glittered as it was a nostalgic moment. Some memories are precious and enduring, they don't fade away easily. As she was going through pictures and cards, she managed to have a glance at a small black and white photograph beneath a greeting card. She slowly pulled it out and looked at it for about a minute or so.

It was her childhood picture, when she was about 7-8 months old. But what made her stare for so long was the picture of a little girl who looked exactly like her. There were two little girls lying in the bed and smiling at each other. Amelia was startled. How can someone look so identical to her and who was she? She didn't know the girl and she had never seen that picture earlier. There were literally inordinate amounts of questions juggling up in her mind.

She rushed to her parents in the living room and asked about the photograph. Their eyes widened as they saw the picture. They looked at each other with uneasiness.

Her mother replied, "Darling, don't you know her? She is your cousin, Lara. You both resembled a lot in childhood." Lara was her aunt's daughter who was just two months elder to Amelia.

Even if it was hard to digest her mother's response, she believed her. After all, why would her mother lie to her? She got up from the sofa and started walking towards her room. Her mother shouted from behind, "Dear, don't forget to wish Lara on her birthday. It's on the 18th, day after tomorrow". Amelia smiled and nodded.

She exactly knew that she would be making a picture collage and posting it on social media. Being a designing student, she could surprise anyone with her creative collages. Amelia gathered all the photographs and started to prepare a collage for her birthday. She preferred doing things on a priority basis because she didn't like to keep things piling on. It took her 15- 20 minutes to prepare the collage. It consisted of all the new and old pictures of them and also, the picture which she discovered so late. She was assured that Lara would also be stunned after witnessing that picture.

Finally, on 18th at 12:00 am, Amelia posted the collage and tagged Lara. She had also written a beautiful caption for her. Within a few minutes, she received a call from Lara. "Amelia, just saw your post. It's so beautiful. Thank you so much. But who is that cute little girl with you? I guess you posted it by mistake. That's why I called you," Lara asked.

Amelia was in extreme ambiguity. "What? I was told that it's you. And I was really amazed to know that we resembled so much earlier." Amelia replied.

Lara giggled a little and said, "Dear, won't I know how I looked earlier? It's not me at all. Wait, let me send you my childhood pictures." They were on the call itself and Lara sent some of her precious old photographs to her. Amelia jumped out of her skin when she realized that the photos didn't match at all with the picture she had. They were totally different.

"I will call you back," Amelia said. She put down her phone and sat down calmly. There were a lot of questions on her mind now. She was bothered by why her parents lied to her? Who was she? Was she her twin sister? She had no clue. But she wanted to get her questions answered. She searched for her birth certificate in her drawer. She took out her old folders and was able to find it. She noted the hospital's address on a paper. She decided to visit that hospital next morning.

The next morning, she dressed up quickly and went downstairs.

"Where are you going?" Her mother asked.

"Umm, I'll be back in an hour mommy, just going to Diana's house to meet her," she replied.

"Be back soon, I've cooked your favourite pasta," her mother said.

Amelia looked for the car keys in the basket. She went to the garage to reach the car. The hospital wasn't very near. It took her about 25 minutes to reach their.

She reached the reception and asked, "May I know where Dr. Smith is?"

"Ma'am, he'll be here shortly," the receptionist replied.

Amelia took a seat and was quite restless. After a wait of 15 minutes, an old man with thick specs and a smiley face arrived at the reception.

"Sir, there's she," the receptionist pointed at Amelia. "Hello sir. I am Amelia Mathews. Actually, 20 years ago, I took birth in this hospital and I wanted to know about something," Amelia said.

"Yes dear, go ahead," the Doctor replied.

"Sir I need to know the details of my birth. Like the timings and other details." Amelia said.

"Sure dear, I will go through the records and let you know by tomorrow. Just let me know your date of birth and the name of your parents." Doctor replied.

Amelia came back home. She was eagerly waiting for the doctor's call. The next morning at 10 am, she received a call from an unknown number. Amelia knew that it was the doctor.

"Hello, yes sir. I was waiting for your call." She said.

"Hello dear. Your mother, Mrs. Lisa Mathews had given birth to twin daughters on 24th April 2000 at 5:18 pm. She underwent a normal delivery with absolutely no complications. I'll be mailing you the full details shortly. Take care." Doctor said.

Amelia was shaken to the core. She already had a doubt that it was her twin sister, but knowing the actual facts and digesting the truth had become next to impossible for her. Where was she? What happened to her? And why did her parents never tell her about this?

But she was too determined to solve this mystery. She definitely knew that her parents were hiding a lot of things. Therefore, she decided to talk to her elder brother, James, who was 8 years elder to Amelia. She went to his room and sat on the bed with an extremely strained face.

James curiously asked, "What happened? You look sad."

"No I am not sad. I just have a question," she replied.

"What? Ask"

"Did I have a twin sister?"

James' face turned pale. He didn't know what to reply. After a few moments he said, "Umm, are you mad? How's that possible?" He hesitated. Amelia pulled out the photograph from her pocket and showed him.

"Then who is this? Why are you all lying to me? I have the proofs, she said.

"What, what proof?" He asked.

"See, the reports. I went to the hospital to collect this! The doctor himself said that our mother gave birth to two daughters on that day."

"Sshh, please lower down your volume. I'll tell you everything but please, be calm." He insisted. Amelia tried to control her vexation.

James started, "I was very little when I saw that. I can't forget that incident. The day when you and your sister were born, I was the happiest of all. But when she was 11 months old, she experienced a rare gene disease which led to paralysis. Everything started becoming abnormal in her body. It became difficult for our parents to handle the situation. They decided to keep a Nanny for you and me because they were totally occupied with that girl. Our parents never allowed me to visit that room. They didn't want me to get attached to her. Two-three months passed this way.

Then one night when we were asleep, I heard some voice from the other bedroom. I witnessed that the light was on and I could see some shadows too. I slowly went towards that room and the thing which I saw then, makes me shiver till today and always will. Amelia, I know that you won't believe me, but our parents killed our sister. They had choked her with a pillow. I couldn't swallow that thing. I was nervous, shocked and dismayed. I couldn't sleep for so many days. Thinking that our parents were the killers of our own sister just broke me to the core. They don't yet know that I am aware of that bitter truth. After she was dead, they dug a pit in our backyard and buried her body. I also remember that they didn't allow me to play there for many days."

Amelia was so shaken that she was numb and quiet. She kept staring at the ground. James looked at her and said, "Please Amelia, never disclose this thing in front of our parents."

"Brother, were not they scared to face everyone else? How can they even do this?" She asked in the lowest voice.

"She was going to die in a few months. That disease was going to kill her soon. But, our parents were so frustrated already, that they couldn't wait for her natural death. They told everyone that she passed away at night when she was asleep but it's not the truth. I am sure that they still regret it, but I decided to forget about everything and move on. I would suggest you to do the same, Amelia. It's good for our family."

Amelia nodded and went back to her bedroom. She definitely wasn't going to question her parents about this, ever. But, the questions imprinted in her soul forever:

Even if she was going to die, was it fair to take away her life?

Even if she gave sleepless nights, would someone kill her for that?

Even if her body wasn't working, her heart was still beating.

Who gives the right to stop her heartbeat? It became difficult for her to talk to her parents for some days. But eventually, her life came back on the track.

SOME WRONGS ARE NEEDED TO BE ACCEPTED AND LIVED WITH.

SOME PUZZLES DON'T GET SOLVED.

SOME INCIDENTS DON'T HAVE EXPLANATIONS.

SOME QUESTIONS REMAIN UNANSWERED.

STORY EIGHTEEN

A REBELLION IN HEAVEN

by CF Gonzi

The sun's golden rays penetrated the purple sky, reflecting brightly off the water of the fountain in the square. Elizabeth halted her chase for just a moment, taking a deep breath of the evening air. Autumn was upon them—Elizabeth's favourite time of the year. Cecil was near to the corner before he realized she was no longer running with him.

"Beth!" His breathing was hard as he beckoned her forward. "We're going to be late!"

Shaken out of her reverie, Elizabeth nodded and rushed forward, catching up to Cecil as he quickened his pace once more.

"It's just such a beautiful evening," Elizabeth tucked a stray hair behind her ear. "I couldn't help but think of the vibrant colours the trees will be turning soon."

"Every evening here is beautiful, Beth," Cecil rolled his eyes. "There's no meeting tomorrow night, waste your time thinking about trees then."

Cecil halted in front of a wooden door, and Elizabeth came to rest beside him as he knocked a rhythmic pattern. The door opened a crack, just wide enough for a brilliant green eye to peek out at the siblings.

"Have you had supper?" The owner of the eye asked in a solemn voice.

"Not enough for our hunger," Cecil answered.

The heavy door creaked open, revealing a staircase lit by glowing lanterns. Elizabeth followed Cecil down, sighing at the obscure exchange. She had been to plenty of these meetings with her brother, and only now was she starting to see why they were so important.

"Excuse me." Cecil was trying to make a path in the sea of people they had met at the bottom of the staircase. "Sorry, excuse me. C'mon, Beth."

Elizabeth held on to her brother's tunic, letting him part the crowd to get a better view of the front of the tavern. For as small as the building looked from the outside, this spacious basement held quite the number of people. If Elizabeth had to guess, she would have estimated about one-third of the kingdom had shown up for this meeting.

"Oi, Cecil!" It was Kenneth, the kingdom's blacksmith and Cecil's mentor. "O'er here, where ya can see better."

Cecil stomped up to the giant of a man, puffing his chest out to make his scrawny frame more impressive. Elizabeth giggled to herself.

"'Ello there, Miss Elizabeth," Kenneth was wide enough to command space around himself, so there was plenty of room for Elizabeth and Cecil to join him. "So great to see ya join the cause."

"It's an exciting time." Elizabeth bit her tongue. She knew better than to say what she really thought, or why she was really there.

"Truer words never been spoken, Miss." Kenneth clapped Cecil on the back, making his knees buckle. "With Prince Lucius leading us, I don' see—ah! Speak o' the devil 'imself."

It was surprising how silent the crowded room had become as the demanding air of royalty fell upon them. Elizabeth stood on her tiptoes, blushing slightly as she watched the glorious man step up onto the crate at the front of the group. He was tall and slender, his hair black as night and his skin as pale as the moon. He had forsaken his royal robes for a heavy maroon tunic, and a magnificent sword lay strapped to his hip. His golden eyes rested on Elizabeth's for a split-second, and she felt her heart thud to her throat.

"My Brothers and Sisters!" Prince Lucius raised his long-fingered hands in welcome. "I am overjoyed to be joined by such a beloved and *large* percentage of my kingdom."

"No' his kingdom yet, though, is it?" Kenneth whispered gruffly. Cecil scoffed.

"As many of you know," Prince Lucius continued as if he had not heard Kenneth, but Elizabeth could have sworn she saw his eyes wash over their little corner once more. "My father, the King, has denied my request to be the conqueror of the land below."

A few people in the crowd hissed at this, Cecil being one of them. The satisfied smile playing on the prince's lips made Elizabeth's stomach flutter.

"He has appointed my eldest brother, Josiah, to this task instead, saying that it is not a conqueror they need, but a saviour." This gained a larger uproar than before; Josiah was not as popular with this class of the kingdom.

"I delight in your loyalty, every one of you." Prince Lucius licked his lips hungrily before continuing. "I fear, however, that this silent rebellion will not be enough to change my father's mind."

Elizabeth relaxed her toes, flattening her feet to the floor. She knew this was coming, but had been so flattered by his words that she chose to ignore the signs.

"I am afraid I will have to ask, plead, and beg if need be, that you all stand, and fight with me." Prince Lucius raised a hand at the growing murmuring in the crowd. "Tomorrow."

Kenneth roared in outrage. "Tomorra? You want us ready for the battle by mornin'? What is this bull—"

Kenneth was drowned out by the thunderous growl of a room full of uneasy people. Elizabeth backed against a wall, watching doubt flood the room. Glancing up at Prince Lucius again, she saw the same sultry smile on his lips, and felt a calm wash over her body. He knew what he was doing, and she just needed to trust him, like she had always done.

Eventually, the room quieted down, more out of curiosity at how the prince would handle the unrest than out of resolution.

"My friends, my Brothers and Sisters," his emphasis was inspiring. To think that someone of royal blood would see these commoners as their family! "I know, it is much to ask. But if we do not act quickly, Josiah will depart without so much as a goodbye, and we will be left with nothing.

"If we incite the battle tomorrow, spring an attack upon those who contradict our wants, my Father will be forced to listen to your voices as I have. He will see the sense in sending *me* to the land below. And you will all be welcome to join me there."

Aside from her unrighteous lust for the prince, the thought of taking part in such a grand adventure was enough to convince Elizabeth that this was the right thing to do. It seemed to be enough for the previously uneasy crowd as well, because people all around her were nodding their heads in agreement.

"We march at dawn." Prince Lucius was clasping his hands in delight, his golden eyes shining through the tavern-like fire. "I will fight with you and for you to the end, my friends."

Elizabeth watched as the prince stepped off the crate and made his way toward her. He was shaking hands with the men and bowing generously to the women, creating an atmosphere of absolute trust in the claustrophobic tavern. Finally, he approached her and her brother.

"Cecil, you brute," Prince Lucius put a hand on Cecil's shoulder. "I am honoured to call you my brother."

The prince's gorgeous eyes turned to Elizabeth, and she felt her knees weaken. Taking her hand in his, Prince Lucius bent low and kissed her fingers lightly. Elizabeth's breath caught tightly in her chest.

"And Miss Elizabeth," he stayed low as he addressed her. "Your support by far means the most."

"It is you who means the most, kind prince." Elizabeth curtsied, curling her fingers into his. "Everyone here would be in agreement."

Prince Lucius smiled devilishly as he squeezed her fingers, and Elizabeth flipped her light hair over her shoulder to expose more of her neck. The prince's eyebrows shot up as he moved closer, but the sound of echoing footsteps froze everyone in the room.

"Castle guards, just outside the alley." The man from the door huffed as he reached the bottom of the stairs. "We must leave right away to avoid detection."

Prince Lucius' face grew solemn as he looked back at Elizabeth.

"Tomorrow," he held her hand tightly. "After all is said and done, we will have our time, my dearest Elizabeth."

Elizabeth's hand was pulled from the prince's as Cecil swept her in with the rest of the horde moving toward the staircase. She stomped up the stairs unhappily and tried her best to put on a nonchalant face as she and Cecil were allowed to enter the kingdom's streets once more.

She couldn't sleep that night, staring at the ceiling of her room till the sunrise as she anticipated the rebellion. Elizabeth had no experience on the battlefield, but she was smart. She hoped to join the prince in the tactical planning of the battle, and was so excited to see him again that she beat Cecil to the door that morning.

"Didn't sleep." He said grumpily as he put on his cloak. "Too much adrenaline for today."

"Same," Elizabeth answered, though hers was completely different adrenaline.

Cecil looked out the window as he took a bite of stale bread. He spit it out, choking loudly.

"What? What's wrong?" Elizabeth ran to her brother.

"Guards," Cecil sputtered. "P-palace guards patrolling the streets."

Elizabeth's eyes grew wide as she peeked out the window as well. Sure enough, the kingdom's insignia was marching up and down the road outside their home.

"How are we supposed to meet up with Prince Lucius if we can't leave our home?" Elizabeth exclaimed.

"We can lie. Get to the prince through an alternate route. C'mon."

Gritting his teeth with the resolve of revolution, Cecil took Elizabeth's hand and led her out the door. Within seconds, metal-clad hands were upon them, tearing them away from each other.

"Cecil!" Elizabeth cried, looking back at her struggling brother.

"What's going on?" Cecil was very convincing. He seemed genuinely confused. "Why are you attacking us?"

"All peasants in this sector are being brought in for questioning," one of the guards rehearsed.

Elizabeth struggled violently, desperately trying to get out of the vice grip holding her and reach her brother.

She couldn't.

Finally submitting, she let herself go limp, and was carried forward, watching through her tears as Cecil continued to fight behind her.

Everything went by in a blur. Eventually, Elizabeth was lowered in the middle of a courtyard behind castle walls, where many, if not all, of the people from last night's meeting were now kneeling on the ground. Cecil was thrown roughly next to Elizabeth, having been bound by strong ropes to stop his struggling. Elizabeth lifted him up to see what the rest of them were staring at.

It was Prince Lucius. Also bound by large chords, kneeling in front of the King's feet. Prince Josiah stood to the right of the king. Elizabeth watched him curiously; she had never seen him before. He looked surprisingly kind.

"Lucius," the King addressed the entire crowd, not even looking at his son. "You stand charged for malicious rebellion and the leading away of the hearts of these, my people. How do you plead?"

"Not guilty." Prince Lucius growled, his charismatic aura gone.

"You deny having planned with these people to rebel against my kingdom?" The king gestured out to all of us.

Prince Lucius' handsome smile was gone. His eyes met Elizabeth's, but his gaze remained hard, and Elizabeth's heart shattered at his next word.

"Yes."

An explosion of outrage and shock sounded all around Elizabeth. She couldn't believe it. She didn't want to believe it. This was just part of his plan. He wasn't betraying them.

"So, you were to do it alone?" The king pressed, raising his voice above the noise of the angry crowd.

"I never had plans to rebel." Prince Lucius glared at his father as the people around Elizabeth began to stand and shout in their rage.

"According to this man, my son, that is not the truth." The king nodded and Kenneth the blacksmith emerged from behind a castle door.

Cecil, who had been screaming in protest, now stood still, staring up at his mentor with glistening eyes.

"You cannot deny now, my son." The king looked solemnly at all of us. "But, if you have an ounce of love for these people you have led astray, you may renounce them, and face the consequence yourself."

Prince Lucius looked out at the uproarious crowd, his eyebrows knit in a long-hidden loathing. Elizabeth's eyes overflowed with tears as she watched the hatred emanating from the man she once loved.

"It's their fault, my king," Lucius spoke softly. "They begged me to lead them. They do not love you. They do not deserve this kingdom."

The king's face fell as the guard's swarmed the now rioting crowd.

"Lucius, for your crimes, you are banished from my kingdom," the king held his staff out, demanding the attention of the prince's followers. "Do you wish to follow him in his misery?"

STORY NINETEEN

THE FACADE

by Rashi Aggarwal

VIEWERS WITNESSED SOMETHING UNNATURAL DURING PRESIDENT'S SPEECH LAST NIGHT

President Mcgerald addressed the nation yesterday at 8 p.m. as he always does on the first day of every month. He telecasted his speech from his residence at the President House because of the global pandemic. The public witnessed something unnatural during his address. President Mcgerald didn't appear like he usually does. President Mcgerald kept switching his appearances between previous presidents' avatars and himself. It looked as if he was shapeshifting. The speech was interrupted by his assistant, stepping in front of the camera and the telecast was terminated. The incident was covered up by the officials stating it as a technical issue.

"Did you read that? The virus has affected you like nobody else. People saw the glimpse of your reality yesterday. I told you not to go on camera. They are this close to realizing your truth and this world's reality," Ronald said as he paced the room nervously.

"I know what I am doing. The centralized system your ancestors built is acting up. They put me in charge to save your world and you are supposed to serve me instead of questioning me. People were already suspicious about me when that light beamed out of my eyes. I haven't given a public appearance since December last year."

***

Once upon a time, the world was tormented by the never-ending famine, vast spreading of various diseases and wars. Millions of animals as well as plant lives disappeared into thin air as a result. Beings which are said to be supernatural in today's world were once a reality. The Earth was walked by witches, gargoyles, shapeshifters, warlocks and what not. There was a time when all stood united and lived together in peace and harmony. Their ancestors created one humongous island so their land stands united like their bond. All was good, till the day a huge meteor hit the centre of the island and created the Gulf of Guinea, known as the 'centre of the world' in today's time. It wasn't an ordinary meteor but a curse from the ones who were more powerful, the ones who lived on the other side of the universe. They inflicted their evil to our world. As the darkness spread, it started consuming life with it. Nature was vanishing.

Blaming each other for the end of the world they fought among themselves, not knowing the extent of their powers. The island, which was nothing less than a heaven, turned into a living hell. The sky turned gloomy, trees were on fire, remaining animals either suffocated to death or died of hunger and thirst. The warlocks are known to create a balance in nature and they worship and respect their ancestors. Seeing how their ancestor's world was disregarded, it enraged them.

Believing the wars as the major cause, they decided to take the matter in their hands. The Ember coven came together to perform the spell which changed everything, some things which were never anticipated. The coven was led by Albeit. When the news reached him, he hit his staff against the land so hard. It caused a catastrophic explosion, something similar to a supernova. The explosion tore the island into several pieces, separated by the deep oceans ruled by deadly creatures. None of the supernatural beings survived it except the Ember Coven and the shapeshifters. Nature was balanced by taking away the powers from the alternative generations. The generations born without the powers were the first humans to step on the Earth and as they multiplied, the magical world became a myth. Soon magic faded away.

The mermaids who came in the proximity of the meteor turned to ash. They exiled to the deepest and the darkest parts of the water as their new home, swearing never to return. Albeit finally reached the root cause, he realised the diabolical nature of the meteor. The coven decided to build a centralized system to control the darkness of the meteor. The darkness was something never experienced and if not controlled, it would be impossible to restore the planet. Albeit decided to put a barrier spell to protect the centralized system. This wasn't an ordinary spell. It required black magic which involved extracting energy from mass killings. The coven trapped all the shapeshifters and got them ready to proceed with the spell. Immense power is released when a shapeshifter is killed because of their ability to have different forms and live several lives.

The coven was able to put the barrier spell so nobody could mess with the system and it remained a secret. The spell was so strong that it killed all the warlocks and witches who performed the spell, including Albeit. Albeit lived long enough to realize that the darkness didn't affect one shapeshifter. The baby shapeshifter floated above the darkness as if the darkness was scared of it. Albeit focused his hand towards the shapeshifter and did a spell before he was consumed by the darkness.

***

Samuel was the blessed one. He was raised by the remaining witches of the Ember coven. He was brought up and trained to be the future leader, living in different disguises. He was given the responsibility to guard the secret of the Gulf of Guinea. Samuel took responsibility and swore to save mankind. The Ember Coven males swore to guard Samuel. The males from Albeit's lineage swore to serve Samuel as his right hand. He was given the gift of immortality by Albeit right before he died.

Samuel was able to restore the world's beauty where humans and animals could live in harmony. He adorned the faces of the world's most powerful leaders. There were hurdles in his way but he always tackled them ferociously. He was Alexander the Great, Ashoka and much more. He evolved as the world evolved

He was able to make the Earth a better place, which was Albeit's vision. It was all good until the present year. There were glitches in the centralized system. The barrier spell was lifted. Since the generation of magical Ember coven came to an end this year, no one could do the spells to restore it again. The spells were forgotten as the centuries passed and magic was erased from the face of the Earth. It was all illusion and a magician's tricks now.

Samuel wasn't the saviour the coven believed him to be. He made the world a living hell for one more time....

The system didn't glitch till he meddled with it. The world went haywire and he is the worst present president.

***

"Ronald! Strange activities are being observed at the centralized system. The portal has opened and black smoke is arising. They are coming! History will repeat!" One of the officials blabbered as she barged into Samuel's office where Ronald paced nervously.

"What are you saying? I'm not getting any of this."

Samuel took out the gun from his drawer. He stood up, aiming his gun at the official and shot her. Since the door closed automatically and the room was soundproofed, no one heard the gunshot. Ronald turned to Samuel in shock, not able to contemplate what he just witnessed.

Samuel walked towards Ronald with his eyes fixated on him. As he walked, he kept switching his appearances into Albeit and the rest of the Ember coven that led to the end of his people. Ronald stood paralyzed. It looked as if he was hypnotised and frozen to one spot by Samuel's gaze. He was standing in front of the most powerful creature in the world and experiencing his wrath

"Albeit killed my family, my people. Then he had guts to pass on his mission to me, making me suffer for centuries. I kept quiet, got trained by your own people and they made me into the strongest being in the world. Ever wondered why magic erased from the face of the Earth? It is because of me, I killed the magical generations, always keeping one person of each generation alive. It wasn't your fault, your family died in an unfortunate fire, you know. It's sad you didn't marry yet. Good for me though, lessened the burden of killing them. I don't need your lineage anymore. After centuries of collecting Ember blood, I was able to reach my goal. I was able to break into the centralized system. The barrier spell is lifted. They are rising and so is the darkness. I will have my family back and this world will be consumed by the darkness. I have avenged them. Nobody will survive the darkness. This world will be ours finally. Only shapeshifters will walk the Earth."

Samuel took out the knife which was tucked in the back of his pants and slit Ronald's throat open.

MEET THE CO-AUTHORS

CF Gonzi

C.F. Gonzi has always had a wild imagination, and she discovered early on that writing was a fantastic outlet for all of her exciting ideas. She currently lives in a beautiful valley with her husband and daughter, where she enjoys rock-climbing, reading, and hiking when she's not writing. UNRAVELED is C.F. Gonzi's debut novel.

Shel Henderson

Shel was born in Oakland, California where he spent the majority of his life, until settling in Manchester, New Hampshire as an adult. As a teen, he found himself fascinated with Middle and Early Modern English, finding the writing language eloquent and captivating. Inspired by such authors such as Mary Shelly, Oscar Wilde and Bram Stoker; this literature has helped shape Shel's affinity for the horror genre in both books and film.

Hari Pudipeddi

Hari is 24, from Hyderabad, currently working as a trainer in procurement. He loves to create and tell stories; writes short fiction and poetry. He reads anything except romance. And is interested in studying philosophy and psychology as a lifelong endeavour.

Dr Anuraag Awasthi

Dr. Anuraag Awasthi is an Educationist, Management Consultant, Trainer, Actor, and author of several books including Amazon Best Seller "Person to Personality in 15 Easy Steps". He has been honoured with Awards like "Rajiv Gandhi Excellence Award", "India Excellence Award", "Shiksha Gaurav Puraskar", "Pride of the Nation", "50 Most Inspiring CEOs", etc. He is a double PhD, with several Masters.

Snehal Agarwal

Snehal Agarwal is a 21-year-old Chartered Accountant from Mumbai. She is talkative, a sitcom fanatic and secretly a nerd. Her stories are a reflection of events commonly occurring around us yet ignored by most. She believes in making a change in the society, one day at a time.

Colby Hobson

Colby has been a passionate writer. Ever since he was young, he's been making stories in his mind and acting them out with Lego's and action figures. Colby's imagination is an endless abyss of ideas for stories, settings, characters, and MUCH MORE! His stories are truly a work of pure genius and he works tirelessly when writing. It's his passion!

Adyasha Mishra

Adyasha Mishra is a BBA graduate from Symbiosis University. She is also pursuing her C.S course from 'The Institute of Company Secretaries of India'. She is a video creator on YouTube and Instagram. Her passion and dedication towards singing, acting, sketching, and writing is eternal and alluring.

Kriti

Kriti is a 21-year-old finance professional. Till the time a story is intriguing to her, the genre doesn't matter. One such fascinating mythological tale inspired her to write her first story years ago. She lost her touch with writing outweighed by her ambitions but now, coming back to it has made her happier than ever.

Suraj Singh Sisodia

Suraj Singh Sisodia has a degree in Mechanical Engineering. He has an interest in creepypastas, history, and lucid dreaming. He enjoys rain and gazing at stars on a clear night. He has worked on numerous projects with All India Radio and Doordarshan for documentaries and ground reports, but his true love has always been writing.

Srishti Sareen

Srishti Sareen organized her plan for her future, about what and how everything she will manage further in her life. She disclosed everything soon enough. About what she had schemed and how she got an opportunity to follow her dreams literally out of nowhere to be worthy enough and be a published author. She is now fulfilling the dream she always craved for. Though sooner than what she actually planned but things are better when they are left unplanned.

Ayush Aggarwal

Ayush Aggarwal is a believer of destiny. He believes that we're all these little parts of a machine constantly working, making sure that we end up exactly where we're supposed to be, when we're supposed to be there. He believes that the universe is, in fact, listening to us.

OUR STORY

We're all on a Journey, and our "Writers" have made it Beautiful.

A dreamcatcher is an object made with feathers and strings, essentially used as lucky charms in many parts of the world. The same way, Inkfeathers brings together writers, editors, and artists together to form a dreamcatcher that works in favour for the young writers and readers and if you're positive about it, it may bring you luck as well.

We at Inkfeathers are connected to thousands of writers globally, who believe in the magic of telling stories. This stream of connectivity with the writers, the fact that everyone has a unique detail or edge to their story makes Inkfeathers proud to partner with these young literary as well as collaborative minds.

Back in 2013, our founders came together to form an offline group for their love of literature, and this formed collaborative energy with many young literature-wounded minds which eventually led these offline meetings to stand-ups, storytelling events, poetry slams, meet-ups to share experiences and many others. In 2016, Inkfeathers finally launched as the brand project under one Private Limited Company. This expanded opportunity gave a number of possibilities and a new way to expand our support for writers.

This dream of wanting to bring together writers as well as readers has come true beyond measure as writers connect to us from countries like United States, United Kingdom, Canada each day to bring their stories to life.

As of this year, we are extremely delighted to provide you our website (www.inkfeathers.com) where all your queries can be resolved about our self-publishing process and latest anthologies. You can get hold of the latest updates on anthologies, events, offers, new book releases and so much more here. You can go ahead and order a book from our bookstore to get a taste of our mindful curation of stories and poems.

Inkfeathers Publishing family encourages you to really put your feelings out there in words for the world to see, in order to have a common ground to grow mutually. We are a creative platform for all those seeking literary help in terms of having their words published.

Believe us, publishing a book is not easy, but we come to a writer's rescue at each phase of having their book in print in terms of Editing, Designing, Branding, Marketing and all the other work that goes behind until you have a printed copy in your hands for Distribution. Together, it couldn't have been any easier. We will be there for you, to help you turn your manuscript into a freshly bound book that sells off the glass bookshelves.

With Love,

Inkfeathers Publishing

OTHER PUBLISHED BOOKS

Hope And Beyond brings some stories of warriors; some real, some fictional who fought an unseen battle, not with a living monster but with something more powerful, our own mind and body. The world is closing and what is most important is to open up to yourself and to have faith in the warm hugs you receive on your way. This book wants to test that power of sharing and test the strength in the stories of acknowledging the heavy and hazy days.

Scan the QR Code
To know more & order your copy.

Taking you on some unplanned, mystical journeys into this realm of 23 beautifully mysterious minds. Little Occult Affairs has everything it takes to keep you flipping through pages trying to envisage each writer's mind and experience life, death, secrets, darkness and so much more as you dive deep in it, making you feel like you live the story itself.

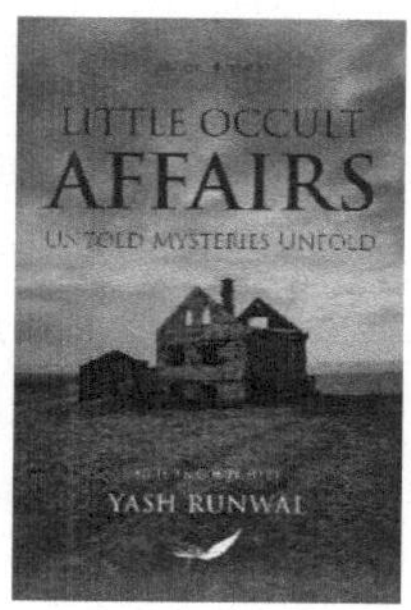

Scan the QR Code
To know more & order your copy.

Forgetting the hustle-bustle of the regular world, let's dive inside a deeper realm that has so many intriguing mysteries to offer. Our heart has a lot to teach us. This book will open your mind towards the untravelled purpose, the undetected significance and the unexplored value which lies within us and around us. LET THE HEART LEAD has everything it takes to make you acknowledge the spirituality that resides in all of our hearts. From "Self Ishq" to "Spirituality", from Spirit Animals to Resonance and from soul mates to twin flames, this book has it all.

**Scan the QR Code
To know more & order your copy.**

Do you feel stuck in your own life? Are you going through the same motions and call it living? Have you lost your joy and desperately crave for much-needed seclusion from everything around? Behest by the malaise of hustle and chaos of big cities, Midnight Writers offers you peace in solitude, a beautiful way to embrace silence. This anthology of poems has familiar and unfamiliar terms and phrases, some modern, some long, and others freshly minted.

**Scan the QR Code
To know more & order your copy.**